More praise for

AMERICAN SALVAGE

"These fine-tuned stories are shaped by stealthy wit, stunning turns of events, and breath-taking insights. Campbell's busted-broke, damaged, and discarded people are rich in longing, valor, forgiveness and love, and readers themselves will feel salvaged and transformed by the gutsy book's fierce compassion."

—*Booklist*, starred review

"Most authors imitate life, while only a few create life. Bonnie Jo Campbell creates 'em, then lets her create-lings live according to their own wills."

—Carolyn Chute, author of *The School on Heart's Content Road*

"A strong collection. The pieces are rich in original detail, and highly atmospheric, while maintaining a satisfying sense of familiar territory, local voices."
—Laura Kasischke, author of
The Life Before Her Eyes and *Lilies Without*

"*American Salvage* is not a book for the cowardly. These daring stories, these desperate characters, would just as soon steal your wallet, break your heart or punch you in the gut than openly admit that redemption is possible during these dark times. But it is just this improbable hope that makes her work brilliant. This is Bonnie Jo Campbell at her bravest and best."

—Rachael Perry, author of *How to Fly*

"At their best these stories reflect what Robert Lowell refers to as 'the grace of accuracy,' which might simply be a way of saying that the voice overall convinces at every turn. By voice I mean personality, and these quirky, surprising, sometimes arcane and visceral and big-hearted stories resonate in ways that keep me nodding. . . . I love the risk of each story and how, in the midst of hilarity, a much more serious concern unfolds so that I'd find myself both laughing out loud and squeezing my heart dry simultaneously."

—Jack Driscoll, author of *How Like an Angel*

"The effect of *American Salvage* is that Campbell's Michigan lingers and cannot be ignored or forgotten."

—*Chicago Literary Scene Examiner*

" 'Beware ye who enter here,' and yet you should and must because the work is so fine and truthful and deeply human. And you will surely know yourself and your world better for having come."

—*Small Press Review*

AMERICAN SALVAGE

ALSO BY BONNIE JO CAMPBELL

Q Road

Women & Other Animals

Our Working Lives (edited with Larry Smith)

AMERICAN SALVAGE

Stories by Bonnie Jo Campbell

For Richard—
I hope you enjoy
these tales from the
other side of town.

Bonnie Jo Campbell

W. W. NORTON & COMPANY
New York · London

Copyright © 2009 by Wayne State University Press,
Detroit, Michigan 48201.

For information about special discounts for bulk purchases, please contact
W. W. Norton Special Sales at specialsales@wwnorton.com or 800-233-4830

Manufacturing by Courier Westford
Book design by Isaac Tobin

The Library of Congress has cataloged the paperback edition as follows:

Campbell, Bonnie Jo, 1962–
American salvage : stories /
by Bonnie Jo Campbell.
p. cm. —
(Made in Michigan writers series)
ISBN 978-0-8143-3412-6 (pbk. : alk. paper)
1. United States—Social life and customs—Fiction.
I. Title.
PS3553.A43956A8 2009
813'.54—dc22
2008051203

ISBN 978-0-393-33919-2 pbk.

W. W. Norton & Company, Inc.
500 Fifth Avenue, New York, N.Y. 10110
www.wwnorton.com

W. W. Norton & Company Ltd.
Castle House, 75/76 Wells Street, London W1T 3QT

1 2 3 4 5 6 7 8 9 0

TO DARLING CHRISTOPHER

Contents

AMERICAN SALVAGE

The Trespasser

The mother jiggles her key in the ancient lock, nudges open the heavy oak door with her shoulder, and then freezes on the threshold. The father steps around her, enters the kitchen of the family cottage—last summer he and his daughter painted these walls sunshine yellow—and drops one of his two bags of groceries onto the linoleum. The thirteen-year-old daughter's mouth glitters with braces. She squeezes her gym bag to her chest and says, "Holy crap."

The stove is burned black, the ceiling tiles above it are scorched, and the adjacent side of the refrigerator is sooted. Bedsheets hang over the windows, one of which has been shattered, the broken glass removed. A faint ammonia smell lingers, and the kitchen garbage can is full of empty Sudafed packages and coffee filters and crumpled tinfoil.

A curly-haired blonde departs unseen through the back door, descends the stairs, and heads for the river. A few days ago, she was one of four intruders in the cottage cooking methamphetamine, but when the three men left last Sunday to go home and get a night's rest before work, the girl hid away in a closet in the daughter's room. The men had not realized that the skinny girl with the ravaged face was only sixteen, and they did not know that she had snagged enough meth during cooking to keep herself going, shooting up, for more than a week.

The family discovers that objects in every room of the cottage have been moved. On the kitchen counter, a configuration of condiment bottles—horseradish sauce balanced atop mustard, stacked atop mayonnaise, with two squeeze bottles of ketchup alongside—is encircled by pastel birthday candles arranged wick to end. Drawers are empty, their contents arranged as shrines on tables and dresser tops and in corners. In the bathroom, medicines and ointments and bottles of pills have been lined up on the sink. Tubes of lip balm cluster around an old glass bottle of Pepto-Bismol upon a green-and-white guest towel draped over the toilet tank. In the center of the master bed sits an ancient nest of twigs containing pale blue robins' eggs (collected and blown by a great-grandmother), which forms a nativity scene with a pair of wooden dolls. A dozen old-fashioned clothespins are laid out side-by-side across the foot of the bed like children at a reunion lining up for the group photo.

Figurines and portraits long invisible to the family on the hallway bookshelf in their old juxtapositions have suddenly reappeared: the rocks painted to look like trolls mingle with the miniature bronze pigs, goats, and dinosaurs. These creatures now gaze upon a framed photo of the daughter with her gymnastics trophy. (The daughter switched from gymnastics to swimming two years ago when she shot up four inches in height, right after this portrait was taken.)

All the objects and framed pictures have been polished with soft cloths, which the trespasser then deposited in the hallway hamper. Piled on top of the hamper are a dozen pretty boxes of facial tissue in gray, blue, and yellow, each box opened, with a few tissues extracted.

The trespasser pretended to be visiting her own family's cottage, pretended that the bones in the faces in the photographs were her inherited bones and that she inhabited this place as naturally as the furniture and relics. Although she was alone during the week, the trespasser rearranged the living room so the old leather and wicker chairs are now turned toward each other, forming a conversation nook instead of facing the TV. She vacuumed the living room and then changed the bag and vacuumed again, sucking up all the cobwebs and even the ash from the fireplace.

At first there seem to be a few objects missing from the daughter's room, but the daughter discovers them in her closet, where the trespasser slept five nights in a nest created from all the pillows in the house. She curled there with two stuffed ponies and a unicorn, the pink flannel pajamas that say *Daddy's Girl*, and the secret purple spiral notebook that is identical to the one the daughter keeps in the city. The trespasser read and reread the notebook in which the daughter has detailed frustration about a poor swim performance and about boys, and at other times has written that she is overwhelmed by pain that feels larger than herself, pain that connects her to girls she never talks to, but only sees from a distance, tough girls she is afraid of, with their heavy eyeliner and the way they glare back at her if she looks too long.

The daughter has made it more than thirteen years without having spent a night with her dresser pushed up against her bedroom door to keep her mother's friends out. Nobody has ever burned her face with a cigarette, and she has never burned her own arms with cigarettes just to remember how terrible it feels. The swimming daughter has never tried to shoot up with a broken needle, never spent time in the juvenile home or in the filthy bathroom of an abandoned basement apartment, has never shaken uncontrollably in the back seat of a car all night long. The daughter has never broken a window to crawl into somebody else's place, has never needed something so badly that she would do anything for three men, strangers, to get it.

The trespasser has been moving along the riverbank, crouching low, and now she comes upon a wooden rowboat belonging to a neighbor. She unties the rope, climbs in, and pushes off before she realizes she has no oars. The current catches the boat, and over the next several hours, she floats downstream. Sometimes the wind catches the boat and it spins.

It is the teenaged daughter, the swimmer, the honor student, who discovers her own missing mattress on the river-side porch, screams "Mommy!" a term she hasn't used in years. The trespasser had dragged the mattress out onto the porch as soon as the men had gone. The daughter studies the sheet, torn off, tangled at one end, the quilted fabric of the mattress crusted with jism, more jism than the daughter's mother has ever seen. The mother takes the daughter's hand, tries to tug her away, but the daughter sees there's blood, too, smeared across the fabric, dried and darkened.

"Don't look," her mother says, but the daughter keeps looking. The daughter inhales the scent of the crime, knows she has walked through the ghost of this crime and felt its chill—in the hallways of her school, in the aisles of the convenience store, and in the gazes of men and women at the Lake Michigan beach where she and her friends swim.

That night, after the trespasser's boat runs aground near a liquor store in a strange town, the daughter goes to sleep in the small bedroom off the kitchen, the room her father jokingly calls *the maid's room*. The dream that scares her awake over and over is the dream of entering a stranger's bedroom—only it is her room—and encountering there her own body, waiting.

The Yard Man

He was standing in mud, leaning on his round-end shovel, when he saw the big orange snake folded on the rocks beside the drive-way, its body as thick as his stepson's arm. Jerry dragged himself out of the waist-deep hole where he'd been digging around the dry well and moved along the side of the building, approached the rocks heel-toe in his mud-caked work boots, trying to move silently in the overgrown grass. The snake was orange with red and gold, but close up, its skin reflected green and blue as well—strangely, the blue of his wife's eyes—and the shiny coils of the snake suggested his wife's coppery hair.

Jerry had seen garter snakes and blue racers and rat snakes here. He had saved the dozen papery skins he'd found and tacked them to the wall inside shed number five, which had recently developed a roof leak and would have to be cleaned out and burned down. But this snake was like no animal he'd seen, as brilliant as the orange butterfly weed that had shot up like flames along the property line a few weeks ago. The snake had a smooth head the size of a Yukon Gold potato, and the look on the snake's face made it seem as if he were smiling in the sunshine. When Jerry was close enough, he reached slowly toward the nearest coil, to touch it.

The shriek caused the snake to uncoil and set out over the rocks, and it made Jerry stand up and knock his shovel into the side of the house, where it chipped a clapboard. His wife, Natalie, stood frozen on the concrete step a few yards away, jaw loose, eyes bulging a little. Her keys jangled as they hit the ground.

The snake moved across the overgrown grass toward the flower garden old Holroyd's wife had planted. It was Holroyd who'd told Jerry the dry well was probably nothing more than a rusted fifty-five-gallon drum of rocks buried outside the makeshift kitchen of the old construction office building where Jerry lived. As usual, Holroyd was right. Maybe Holroyd had been the one to bury it there twenty years ago.

"Jerry!" his wife screamed. "Do something!"

Jerry watched the snake's middle part disappear under the garden phlox, then the hollyhocks. The snake was at least as long as Jerry was tall.

"Kill it!" she shouted. "Jerry, please!"

His stepson and stepdaughter appeared in the window, looking scared, although probably more by their mother's screaming than by a snake they couldn't see.

Jerry picked up his shovel. As his wife of a year and a half had grown more unhappy with him, he'd tried to do whatever she wanted. Had she told him to do the dishes, he would have wiped his hands on his jeans and gone inside to run soapy water, dry well or no dry well. He pursued the snake into the hollyhocks, raised the shovel high enough to slice its body clean through. He didn't know exactly what went on inside a snake's body, but he could imagine a man or a boy chopped in half, how the organs and intestines would fall out. Jerry hesitated, lost sight of the snake in some ground cover, and then saw orange and gold bunching up between flowering bushes. He lifted his shovel again. He could feel his eight-year-old stepson staring at his back.

"For the love of God, Jerry!" his wife screamed, as though the whole ground around them were writhing with snakes. He couldn't blame her—what she felt was as natural as the snake's enjoyment of the sunshine on rocks, as natural as the snake's slipping away from the sound of screaming.

Jerry lifted his shovel and jammed the blade deep into the soil eighteen inches from the snake, which kept sliding away, unaware it had come near death. Jerry studied the line of Indian-corn colors as the snake moved over a railroad tie at the far edge of the garden, into tall, dense grass.

"Did you get it?" she shouted. Her empty hand was grasping at the air.

"Listen, Natalie, honey."

"Jerry, please, at least step on it."

He left his shovel standing upright and returned to her empty-handed, watched her eyes as they changed from terrified to desperate and then to disappointed.

"Oh, honey," he said. "It was too big to step on."

"Why can't you do anything for me?"

"Maybe it's something rare, honey. It's not like any snake I've seen." He wanted to say more, but talking about the beauty of a snake didn't seem right with her being so scared of it.

"Oh, Jerry," his wife said. She turned away from him and spoke toward the hayfield next door. "I'm sorry I can't love every living thing the way you do. I'm never going to love a snake. Or a bat." She laughed a little. "To be honest, I can't even stand that old guy Holroyd you like so much."

Her bra strap pressed into her flesh beneath her tight, thin T-shirt in a way that made Jerry wonder if it might be painful, but he liked watching her muscles flex and relax. He liked the way the snakes of hair in her ponytail curled away from one another as though trying to break free. At another time, he might have defended Holroyd.

"Maybe we need to go on a vacation, you and me," Jerry said to his wife's shoulder. Her neck looked long and pretty with her hair pulled back.

"We can't afford a vacation."

"We couldn't afford one this spring, but we took the kids to Cedar Point." Jerry knew she was right, though. The school had cut Jerry from full-time custodial to part-time this year; the pay cut was devastating, but he'd worked there for ten years, since graduating from the place, and he hadn't yet been able to fathom getting another job.

"Do snakes live in those sheds?" she asked, turning farther away from him and nodding toward the first row of old wooden buildings a hundred yards to the north. "Maybe in those piles of junk?"

"I don't think so," Jerry said. "I think snakes live in the ground."

"I've never lived in a place with snakes, Jerry," she said. "The thought of a snake coming into the house scares the hell out of me. And that bat did get in our bedroom somehow."

"I know. I'm sorry. I'm going to patch the holes in the clapboards. I asked the old lady if she'd pay for new vinyl siding, and she hasn't said no yet."

His wife went inside, let the screen door scrape shut behind her. That metal-on-metal sound was a reminder to Jerry that he needed to screw down the doorframe more securely. He'd installed it last year, but hadn't gotten around to finishing the job. The old lady who owned this place was often willing to pay for materials for home improvements so long as Jerry provided the labor. She seemed to have more faith in Jerry's abilities than he had. When Jerry had lived here alone, he hadn't seen any need to fuss about such improvements. Now he was discovering that every project took longer than expected, and he always wished he'd gotten started earlier. He returned to digging out the dry well.

Four days later, while Jerry's wife was at Campbell Lake with the kids, Holroyd stopped by. As usual, he drove to the top of the property, beyond the white pines, to check for deer tracks—as hunting season approached, he did so with increasing frequency—and then returned and parked and dropped the tailgate of his Ford truck and sat on it. Jerry had gotten the water turned off to the bathroom upstairs, and for two hours he had been staring at the pipes and fixtures, trying to decide how to proceed. He'd never done any serious plumbing, and he was nervous about tearing out the wall. When he saw Holroyd, he called it quits and came down and sat on the other side of the cooler Holroyd had dragged out onto the tailgate. Holroyd handed him a beer; the man's outstretched arm shook as though it had developed a palsy.

"How you doing with them credit cards?"

"Trying not to put anything new on them," Jerry said.

"Good boy. Now get 'em paid off. They'll drag you down, those credit cards."

Jerry didn't want to think about credit cards now, seeing how he and his wife were about to go on a weekend vacation. Instead he looked out over the scrubby field scattered with locusts and maples, and dotted with the storage sheds, rusted hulks of defunct cranes, and piles of deteriorating I-beams and concrete blocks. Way up beyond the white pines, out of sight, was the open, hilly land full of bristly mosses, ground birds, deer, and wild turkeys, even. Jerry didn't bring up the issue of hunting when he talked with the nephew of the old lady who owned the place. He knew she gave him free rent here for insurance purposes; Holroyd had told him if nobody was here to keep an eye on the place, they wouldn't be able to get liability insurance at all.

Jerry said, "I saw a snake the other day, six foot long, at least. Red and orange and gold. Never saw anything like it."

Holroyd nodded, seemed to gasp for air before taking another draw on his cigarette. Jerry had quit smoking before getting married, although he'd had a brief relapse when his old dog, Blue, died a month after the wedding.

Jerry said, "Maybe it was somebody's pet snake got loose."

Holroyd exhaled. "I didn't figure they'd be here anymore."

"What do you mean?"

"You know Red Hammermill. Well, when he moves out and I move in, he tells me about this kind of snake, he draws a picture, tells me keep an eye out for 'em. Of course, you can't believe half of what Red says."

Jerry said, "It was coiled up on the rocks there. Scared the hell out of my poor wife."

Holroyd snorted. Jerry knew Holroyd didn't think much of Jerry's wife or anybody's wife, his own included. Holroyd had been Jerry's ma's boyfriend for a while, though, and he'd treated Jerry nicer than any of the other men his mother dated.

Holroyd had been the yard man for eighteen years, until he married his second wife. She lasted about six months in this place before moving out. Holroyd still seemed surprised at his own decision to follow her. That was five years ago. Now, when Jerry asked, "How's the trailer park?" Holroyd would say something like, "Oh, it's yapping dogs and too many kids and foul food cooking." Or he'd complain, "Everybody's garbage is all pressed up against you in that place, and you've got to hear everybody else's business."

Jerry wouldn't say it, but Holroyd didn't look capable anymore of doing the yard man job, which was more than mowing and trimming and spraying the poison ivy; sometimes Jerry had to load up trailers full of metal to sell as scrap or broken concrete to recycle at Consumers. Last month Jerry had delivered piles of insulation to the hazardous-waste folks, and then there was the business of emptying and burning the old sheds one by one as they became unsafe. More than half of the buildings were gone now, and there were twenty or so concrete block foundations being reclaimed by the earth out there. Jerry was supposed to keep everything trimmed and clear around the sheds, but it was becoming more difficult, with plants and critters creeping in.

"Red said there were a dozen of them snakes at least. Don't know if you can believe what he says. I never saw one, but I didn't go looking. Said the men who worked here sometimes found the snakes coiled up on their crane and dozer engines in the mornings."

"On their engines?" Jerry asked.

"For warmth."

The next day when Jerry got home from working at the school, he found that Holroyd had stuck a dog-eared *Michigan Field Guide to Reptiles and Amphibians* inside his storm door. On the first page was written in a cramped cursive, "R. Hammermill." Also stuck in the door was an envelope containing a check with the reference line, "June—Yard Man," for his ten hours of labor last month. Jerry was sorry to have missed Holroyd, but not the old lady's nephew. The nephew usually wore a suit when he came out with Jerry's check, and the guy surveyed like an investor the thirty-some-odd acres fanning out behind the office building of the old Mid-American Construction Company. Jerry figured that when the old lady died, the nephew would sell this whole place to developers for a bundle, and they'd clear out the buildings and equipment in a few months and build a subdivision. Jerry doubted any big snake would survive.

Instead of getting right to work on the bathroom or patching the holes in the clapboards outside the bedroom, he sat out on the tailgate of his own truck and enjoyed the hazy afternoon, took in a view of the sheds—all painted barn red, although on some the paint was peeling—and he thumbed through the pages with the color pictures of snakes. There were faded notes handwritten on the page showing rat snakes, and somebody had circled the phrase "wide color variation." Jerry wasn't sure about the head; that smiling potato head had looked a little different, but not too different. Six foot was the longest a rat snake got. Jerry flipped through the pages, hoping for the drawing Hammermill had given Holroyd, but it wasn't there. He knew he ought to go inside and get going on that bathroom, or he ought to do some trimming outside, but he poked around the property instead, walked slowly around the sheds, searched the ground for snakes, saw a couple of nests in the grass where he'd let it grow too long. One nest had three speckled eggs in it.

Jerry and his wife headed up north a week later to a resort they could not afford, saw tall pines shaped like palm trees, saw shore birds at the edge of the pond outside their hotel window. Jerry couldn't get enough of seeing the birds come in for a landing with their legs dangling. Jerry and his wife rode the water slide, and he clamped his arms and legs tightly around her as they flew down. He missed the kids, especially his stepson, who would have loved the water slide, and he was glad when his wife said, "We should have brought the kids." Both nights they drank too many sweet drinks, got too drunk to make love, and on Sunday morning, when his wife had a headache, he was glad they had an excuse to go home early.

Once they were on the road, his wife suggested they wait until the evening to pick up the kids from her parents' house. Jerry recalled how when they were first together, when he first got his license, he'd driven her around in his old pickup truck with the bench seat. He'd felt easy pulling her over next to him, and his arm had gone around her long hair, which had felt cool against his skin on hot nights.

They stopped at a tourist shop before getting on the highway for the last stretch, and he bought deer jerky, and she bought what turned out to be a gift for him, a chocolate in foil, and he wished he had bought her something special. He held out the plastic bag of jerky, forgetting she wouldn't touch venison, and she shook her head no. She smiled, though. "It's nice to get away," she said. "The air seems fresher up here."

"How's your headache?" he asked. She looked pretty with the forested hills behind her and the two big rigs dieseling nearby— fortunately the wind was blowing their exhaust in the other direction. He looked at her coppery hair and wanted to ask if she remembered anything particular about that snake, whether he had imagined the great length of the thing, the brilliance of its colors, but the snake was something that he and his wife would probably never talk about.

"The Tylenol helped," she said and smiled again, as though finally she were warming up after a long cold spell.

"It's nice to get away, and it's nice to go home," Jerry said. He was glad to be returning to the yard house, to the queen-sized bed in the room they had renovated before their wedding. His wife had painted the outside edges of the floor around the carpet remnant, and she had chosen all the colors and fabrics, while he had patched the walls and replaced ceiling tiles.

"I'm sorry I get impatient with you, Jerry. It's just that living at a salvage yard is not where I expected to be. It's nice getting free rent, I know, but maybe we need to be thinking about the future."

"I know."

"Maybe if there was at least a fence up so we didn't have to look at the sheds or the piles of junk."

"I can ask the old lady about a fence."

The previous night at the hotel, he'd had a dream he couldn't tell her about, a nightmare in which he'd cut the big snake in half. He'd thrust his shovel into the dirt and the snake had moved, slipped its curving body under the blade. He had watched its organs spill out, saw its innards glisten like egg yolks and Mandarin orange segments in a pudding of dark blood. He'd sliced through the snake so the tail-half was a severed dead thing, leaking guts, and the head-end was writhing in agony, its golden eyes mad with pain. In his dream, the snake's body had become as thick as his son's middle, then as thick as his wife's waist. He had awakened in a sweat, despite the hotel's air conditioning. He had not wanted to disturb his wife, so he'd gone out and paced in the parking lot, where he heard nighthawks diving and whistling. He knew about nighthawks from Holroyd, knew that dusk to dawn they flew over the yard house and fields hunting for bugs, screaming shrilly, although it wasn't anything you'd hear over the sound of the TV if you had it on.

As they pulled into the driveway, he searched for the orange snake. His wife was humming absentmindedly—he liked it when she hummed, changing from one old pop tune to another—and he recalled the way they had clung to each other on the water slide. They carried only the cooler and her purse to the front door, leaving everything else in the minivan. She rested her hip against the doorframe and gazed at him languidly while he fumbled with the key. Before they'd left home, his wife had insisted they make the bed, and so, in a few minutes, when they went upstairs, it would feel something like a motel bed. And his wife would go into the bed with her cool coppery hair and soft thighs and smooth arms, and there would be no children there to disturb them. He would slide over her and inside her and the sunlight would play on them through the curtains, dappling her body. On this hot afternoon, the red squirrels would sleep and not scratch inside the walls as his wife's hair coiled on the pillow. Let snakes sun themselves upon rocks, let spiders suck juices from the bodies of flies they had captured in the night and drop the crumpled corpses to the floor like the shells of tiny pistachios. Let dilapidated wooden sheds settle while weed roots nudged into cracks in their foundations. Let all of nature continue its parade while he made love with his wife, the great love of his life, whom he'd lost in high school and miraculously found again.

The house smelled salty, or sweet, when they entered. Different, anyhow. Jerry wondered if he had left food out. Natalie, too, wrinkled her nose. He decided the smell was both salty *and* sweet.

When his wife went into the bathroom, Jerry pushed open the kitchen door, and the scent became stronger. He looked into the enameled designer sink that his wife's parents had paid for—the old woman who owned the house offered to pay for only the cheapest replacement sink—and found the basin three inches deep in dead bees, thousands of dead bees. What on earth?

Jerry knew his wife should not see the bees. She wouldn't understand—not that Jerry understood. He began to scoop the yellow-and-black bodies into a paper bag with a cup.

"What the hell are you doing?" she asked from the kitchen doorway, her voice alarmed.

She was right to blame him, he thought. These were his bees somehow, his wasted little bodies. Without realizing it, he had probably killed the bees, just as he could easily have killed the orange snake in the garden by misjudging the winding and unwinding of its body.

He picked up a dead bee and studied it in his palm, studied its yellow and black stripes and slightly furry body.

"Let's call an exterminator," she said.

"It's Sunday. And Natalie, honey, they're already dead."

They both looked up and saw live bees buzzing around the light fixture where the ceiling was cracked.

"They look like wasps," she said.

"I'm pretty sure these are honeybees," he said. "I don't think you're supposed to kill them."

"I can't live with bees in my house."

She looked desperate, and he began to understand that this time he had to give in. He had not killed the snake for her, but he would have to sacrifice something. In order to save his marriage, he might have to poison the living bees.

"I wonder if they made honey in our house somewhere," Jerry said. "Wouldn't that be something?" He wanted to plunge his fingers into the sink and take up a handful of dead bees to show her, but instead he held out the single bee in his palm and stepped toward her. He wanted to share this mysterious tragedy with her, but she stepped away from him.

"With all those god-forsaken sheds out there, why do bees have to come in here? I'm calling the exterminator."

"No, honey. Give me one day." He realized the strangeness of calling his wife *honey* just then.

His wife joined the kids at her parents' house. It was summer, after all, and nobody had to be up in the morning except Jerry, to prepare the football field for August practice. His wife was working only a few hours a week this summer, assisting with the school's Friday-afternoon parks program—during the school year, she worked half-days as an administrative assistant in the school office. Jerry drank four beers that night, but resisted smoking, although he got the urge bad. The following morning, he visited the high school biology teacher at home. The teacher confirmed the bees were honeybees, and they contacted a beekeeper. Things started to make sense after that. Jerry called his wife once a day, and after three days, he'd almost convinced her to come and meet the beekeeper who would collect the bees. "Honey, these are something special," he said to her on the phone the fourth day, forgetting again not to call her *honey*. "The beekeeper needs them." He didn't mention that he was going to have to pay fifty dollars to get the beekeeper to come out.

"I won't live in a house with bees," she said again, but she was sounding more lighthearted, and she complained about the way her mother was fussing over what the kids ate. Right before hanging up, she said, "I love you, Jerry, but I do want to have a nice house someday, one I can keep clean, and a nice yard."

"I'll get back to work on the bathroom," Jerry said. He understood her tone to mean she would give him another chance.

The day before the beekeeper came, Jerry went to lunch at the in-laws'. Jerry liked having a father-in-law, although the man seemed to disapprove of Jerry's job, more so since the school had cut him to part time. (Natalie's first husband worked in computers, and, luckily, the kids were still covered by his insurance.) Her parents seemed happy to have their only daughter and their grandchildren near them, but Jerry could tell his wife was getting restless staying there. His wife had been indulged by her parents, had had an upbringing very different from his own, but it wasn't something anybody decided for themselves, how they'd be raised, no more than a hive of bees or a snake decided how it would be raised.

Jerry watched the kids playing in the lush grass of the fenced-in backyard, and the smallness of that green space made him uneasy. His in-laws owned another lot behind this one, which would have doubled the size of their place, but they didn't extend their fenceline to include it.

Jerry shook hands with the beekeeper, who wore a beard, a feed cap, and overalls, and invited him into the house. His words were largely a variety of grunts, and right away Jerry felt at ease with him, the way he'd always felt at ease with old men like Holroyd or Red Hammermill—talking to Red always made him wish he'd had a grandfather.

"Can we cut a hole in your floor or wall," the beekeeper asked, "if we need to?"

"Sure," Jerry said, although, as he climbed the stairs, he felt less than sure. He was glad his wife hadn't shown up. He should have poisoned the bees, no doubt. What had he been thinking? That the bees could be lured out one by one and their hive and queen, too, without destroying anything?

"You got a beer?" the beekeeper asked.

"For catching the bees?"

"For drinking. I don't drink at home, so I like to have a beer when I go out."

Jerry went back downstairs and retrieved two from the refrigerator, although it was only eleven in the morning.

"I need to watch and see where they go," the beekeeper said. They sat on Jerry's unmade bed. Good thing his wife wasn't there. She'd have hated having this man with the greasy Carhartt overalls sitting on the edge of her sheets. The bees followed one another under the bedside stand. Without speaking, the two men moved the bed and nightstand and sat there in silence, drinking their beers, watching until they were sure where the line of bees was entering, through a gap under the baseboard.

"Right around here," the beekeeper said. He moved his hand over the wall. "You can feel the heat in this spot."

"I just boarded up some holes in the siding a few days ago. A bat got in here, upset my wife." Jerry placed his hand on the wall and was impressed by the warmth.

"You must've trapped the bees in the wall."

"Damn. I never considered that."

Jerry volunteered his own reciprocating saw when the beekeeper's keyhole saw seemed slow, but the beekeeper said a power saw would drive the bees crazy. The beekeeper cut a rough rectangle from the quarter-inch painted plywood; when he pulled the swath from the wall, it was piled with wax and honey. All the bees that had been hovering inches away flew toward the honey and stuck themselves there.

"See how they cling?" the beekeeper said. He gripped the hunk of wood. "That means we have the queen. Your job is to take my little dust vac and suck up any of those fellows that haven't stuck themselves to the hive." Most of the bees followed the man making his way slowly down the stairs (honey dripping on the steps), but Jerry traveled around the bedroom, and the whole house, gathering up every wayward bee. The vacuum had been modified to suck gently, and the work was satisfying. Jerry retrieved hundreds of bees from the bedroom, dozens from the kitchen, a few from the bathroom.

"You want another beer?" Jerry asked.

"I'd better not," he said. "I'd better get these bees home. Say, what you got in those sheds?"

"All sorts of construction salvage," Jerry said. "Old building materials mostly."

"When I was a boy, this was a going concern. Mid-American Company, wasn't it?"

Jerry nodded and felt inexplicably proud. As the man was getting into his old truck with the utility cap on it, Jerry asked, "Hey, have you ever heard of a big orange snake in these parts? Orange and red and gold? As long as a man is tall?" Jerry found he didn't want to let the beekeeper go. He wondered about Holroyd, hoped Holroyd would stop by sometime soon so he could tell him about the bees. He wondered if maybe something had happened to Holroyd, for he hadn't seen the man in a couple weeks. Would Holroyd's wife know to call and tell Jerry if something did happen? He'd known Holroyd since he was a kid, since Holroyd used to take his ma to the Pub and sometimes sleep over. It would've sounded odd to say it out loud, but Holroyd was the closest thing he had to a father.

The beekeeper said, "No, nothing like that. I've got your hog-nose snake over by my place, and I once seen a king snake, but nothing like what you're describing."

"They used to be around this place," Jerry said. "A long time ago, and they meant something to people here."

A few days after the beekeeper's visit, to Jerry's surprise, the nephew came by with the report that the old woman would pay for new siding and windows. Jerry visited his in-laws again with a page of samples and invited his wife to choose the siding, and he hid his disappointment when she picked an off-white color called "Desert Rose." (He'd been hoping for dark green.) Even that snake, with its orange and red and gold, somehow fit in with the natural colors, the way a beautiful woman like his wife could still look like a member of her otherwise ordinary family, but the pinkish hue seemed off to Jerry.

He and his wife had been living apart for more than two weeks, but their separation didn't feel permanent to Jerry. His wife spoke warmly to him each day when he called, and with each day he assured her that he was working hard. Putting up the siding gave him respite from the upstairs bathroom, which he hadn't started on yet.

The minivan pulled into the driveway while Jerry was installing siding on the west end of the building, and the kids tore out and ran into the house. A few minutes later, while his wife was standing below the ladder talking to him, he spied a big orange snake. It lay curved like a long easy tongue of flame around a railroad tie at the far edge of Holroyd's wife's garden, and Jerry wanted more than anything to climb down and make his way to the creature. He wanted to glimpse the belly, to see if it was a checkerboard black-and-white or mottled like Indian corn, or if it was blotchy like the top of the snake, but he didn't dare look again in that direction for fear his wife's gaze would follow his. His wife threw back little coils of coppery hair—curlier and shorter than the last time he'd seen her—and said she was sick of living with her parents, said how nice it was out here, with the view over the hayfield, asked Jerry if he'd seen deer out there (he had), asked if he would consider planting evergreens (sure, he would). Her parents had a hedge of yew bushes, and a hedge sure would look nice over there, she said. "It would help block the view of those sheds."

Jerry stole a glance at the garden, but saw only a line of color disappearing. Then he stared at his wife's suntanned throat, her shoulders, her blue eyes and small ears, studied her as he wanted to study the snake. Back in high school, they used to go to Campbell Lake and lie on the sand, and when she closed her eyes to soak in the sunlight, Jerry had stared at her body, her belly, her breasts, her neck, and that glistening hair, streaked by the sun. Summer was not his season, but he'd loved it when she swam, when she threw herself into the water and flipped over on her back and waved at him. With her gold-and-copper hair she looked like a mermaid with a Michigan forest rising behind her.

"Are you okay?" she said.

"I'm fine. Why do you ask?"

"I don't know," she said. "You seem worried, and you're staring at me in that creepy way."

"I guess I'm just tired. I worked at the school this morning," he said. "And the sun's been pretty hot out here. Did you cut your hair?"

"I got a trim and some layers. It's too hot for long hair."

"It's above your shoulders."

"You don't like it?"

"No. I do." If his wife would go to the store right now, or if she'd even go inside the house, he could search the weeds for the snake. Instead, she produced a lawn chair and a thermos from the van, parked herself nearby, and sipped a cool drink.

"Today was the last day of Friday kids' camp," she said. "Thank

God that's over. Those kids have way too much energy. Six parents sent the kids in with cupcakes or cookies this morning, and everybody was bouncing off the walls. I mean bouncing off the trees, since we were out in the park."

He felt guilty for wishing her away. He said, "I'm so glad you and the kids are here."

"Do you want a drink?" she said. "You don't look so good."

"I'm fine." He could feel the snake moving farther away, perhaps in response to his wife's voice.

"You're probably dehydrated. Here, take a drink." His wife brought him her glass, held it up. She continued holding it toward him until he descended the ladder, accepted the glass and took a long draw. He *was* thirsty. Lemonade with artificial sweetener, not the kind of thing he'd go out of his way to drink, but not so bad. He'd drunk worse. He could use a beer, but probably that wouldn't be a good idea, seeing how he was working on a ladder.

She poured herself more from a Thermos, returned to her chair, and put on sunglasses. He climbed back up and looked in the direction of the snake, but didn't see anything. The sun moved west as he worked, and finally, when he couldn't lift his arms one more time, he put away his tools for the night. The kids seemed happy to have their own rooms again after their time cramped with the grandparents—they didn't fight once all evening—and after they'd gone to bed, he and his wife made love for the first time in more than a month. Jerry had pushed the nightstand against the wall to hide the damage done by the beekeeper, but he couldn't sleep for feeling aware of that hole. During the night, he felt certain his wife, too, must be aware of it. Anything could move into that empty space and lurk there, a bat or a squirrel or bugs or some awful part of himself, maybe.

The following day, while his wife was at the beach with the kids, he took some time off from siding the house and used his jigsaw to cut a piece of sheathing that more or less fit the hole—it took him almost two hours to get it right, and he had to add pieces of two-

by-four to the studs to have something to nail into. He lamented
that he hadn't asked the beekeeper about getting the original piece
of wood back. Unfortunately he didn't have quarter-inch plywood,
but used instead three-eighths-inch OSB, so it stuck out a little.
After he nailed it in place, he regretted not painting the piece before installing it—now he couldn't finish it without Natalie smelling the paint.

Over the course of two weeks, he insulated and sided the west
and south sides of the building, and replaced the windows and
trimmed them out. One morning his wife got up early and made
him scrambled eggs for breakfast. He'd heard rumors of more job
cuts at the school, but he didn't ask if she would still have her half-
time office job, didn't want to admit how much they would need
the money.

"I'm happy to be back with you, Jerry," she said as she placed the
eggs and toast already spread with grape jelly before him. "It feels
more like a home with the siding on. The green looks better than I
thought it would. Maybe things will just keep getting better from
here on."

"I should be able to finish it before school starts." He had lied,
told Natalie the old woman had insisted on the green siding.

Jerry's stepson appeared in the doorway, rubbing his eyes.

"I'm so glad you came home, honey," Jerry said to his wife. He
kissed her mouth and called his stepson over for a hug. He heard
his stepdaughter walking around her bedroom upstairs. He closed
his eyes so as not to stare at his wife's face the way she hated.

Things went fairly well throughout the first few months of the
new school year, even though his wife had indeed lost her job to
budget cuts, and they had to take out a loan from her parents to
pay the credit card bills. Jerry's stepson's science project on spiders
received an honorable mention for the top award, although he was
only in third grade. A few people had done moths, but nobody had
captured spiders and displayed their legs so well. The boy had been
frustrated at first when he realized the spider legs sometimes came

loose in the process. Jerry didn't think he had overreached his parental authority by helping the boy reattach the legs with tweezers and rubber cement or in helping catch and asphyxiate the spiders.

"Jerry, they liked the spiders," his stepson whispered during the judges' announcements. They were in the gymnasium of his elementary school. "I know Mom hates them, but the judges liked them."

"Your mom doesn't like a lot of things, son," Jerry whispered. He meant to add something nice. In truth, his wife had done a remarkable job of tolerating the spider project, which they worked on in shed number eighteen, the shed with fifty or so old toilets stored in it. The white porcelain seemed to attract spiders, or at least it made them more visible.

"What's that supposed to mean?" she asked Jerry. The judges were still announcing the special mention prizes. "That I don't like a lot of things."

"We were talking about the spiders."

"Spiders are fine outside. As long as I don't have to see them or come near them or have them touch me."

"Spiders catch lots of flies," the boy said. "They help us."

"I guess that's what your stepfather would say. He loves all the creatures."

Her response seemed prickly, but her smile afterward was genuinely friendly, and when Jerry kissed her on the side of the head, she laughed a little.

Next time Jerry saw Holroyd, the sycamore and sugar maple leaves shone orange and red and gold. Holroyd had trouble lifting himself onto the tailgate, and he was breathing heavily when he lit his first cigarette.

"We going to bag a couple deer this year?" Holroyd asked.

"Sure." There was no shortage of deer on the property, but Jerry wondered if Holroyd could really aim a gun, the way he was shaking.

"You know Hammermill died, right?" Holroyd said.

"No."

"Died three weeks ago. My wife saw the notice in the paper, but I didn't make it to the funeral. I planned to, but I didn't make it."

"Aw, damn." Jerry had enjoyed Red's stories, whether or not they were true. Jerry thought Holroyd's eyes were watering under that hank of white hair.

"I guess that means you and me are the only yard men left," Holroyd said. "The only people who know this old place. My wife can't figure out why I've got to come out here all the time. She's happy with her lawn the size of a postage stamp and her trailer full of knick-knacks and air freshener crap. I can't hardly breathe in that place."

"There's the old woman's nephew." Jerry felt a lump in his throat. "He comes around."

"Aw, that fool-in-a-suit doesn't know shit." Holroyd shrugged. "You know, I always wanted to try and get maple sap out of them sugar maples. Maybe next year we ought to do that, you and me. Collect the sap, boil up some maple syrup in shed number five. There still that old wood stove in there?"

Jerry nodded. He didn't have the heart to tell Holroyd that the old woman sent instructions to sell the wood stove for scrap in preparation for burning the structure. Instead Jerry asked, "Why does the woman keep this place? She could sell it for a lot of money."

"You know how women are, holding onto strange ideas and strange trinkets." Holroyd had to rest his beer on the tailgate when he spoke.

"Can't think of seventeen buildings and thirty acres as a trinket, can you?" Jerry hoped his wife wouldn't get back right away. If she pulled in the driveway, Holroyd would make quick work of leaving.

"Hammermill had a theory," Holroyd said. "He said the old lady worked in her grandpa's company as a girl, fell in love with some job superintendent who was killed in an accident. Hammermill used to claim the woman came to visit him sometimes. *Visit him*, if you know what I mean."

"Was she married? The old lady?"

"Far as I know, she never got married. Far as I know, Hammermill made the whole thing up."

"When I didn't see you for a month there I got worried," Jerry said.

"Yeah, they dragged me up to that goddamned hospital, lousy sons of bitches."

"I wonder if I ought to get your phone number."

"Don't bother. The phones are ringing off the hook all through that trailer park. I don't want to add to the noise."

"I suppose when the old lady dies or when these sheds are all burned down and all the piles of materials are gone, they won't need me," Jerry said.

"Only seventeen sheds left?"

"Sixteen plus the house. I don't know if I could do what you did, move into a trailer park."

"We all do what we've got to do."

"We looked at a prefab in Indiana," Jerry said. "We walked through it on the sales lot."

"Whose idea was that?" Holroyd asked and laughed.

Jerry understood why his wife wanted to live in a prefab. The yard house wasn't carpeted, and the walls here were old wood paneling full of nail holes instead of smooth drywall. Good enough for him, of course; in fact, he preferred a beat-up house to a nice one where he had to worry about wiping his shoes before he came inside or taking them off like at his in-laws'. Jerry said, "The prefabs have low energy costs, and they're easy to keep clean."

Holroyd blew out air in a snort.

Sitting there on the tailgate, Jerry looked around, wished he could see something like white-tailed deer grazing, a mother and a spotted fawn. Life was always out there, he knew, but he'd have to sit still and listen awhile before he'd hear critters munching or rustling or hissing, before he'd see flies being devoured by spiders or see one of them big orange snakes. He wondered, if he listened hard enough, would he hear the dinosaur-like bones of old construction equipment rusting, wooden sheds rotting, sheets of insulation dissolving, piles of old toilets sinking into the ground?

Jerry said, "You think maybe them orange snakes live up top? Maybe they eat birds' eggs up there."

"We can watch for 'em when we're hunting. There's lots of deer tracks this year. Maybe you'll get a deer, too. You get your license yet?"

Jerry nodded, cracked open a second beer from Holroyd's cooler. Usually Holroyd shot two, one for each of them. The sun was setting in a pretty way. If only they could all remain together forever like this, he being the yard man, with his wife and the kids, and Holroyd stopping by to visit. And snakes and bees and deer and ground birds and nighthawks could all stay here with them, and those snakes would stay out of his wife's line of sight, and she would relax and start to love this place the way he did.

And maybe that would have happened. That was one way it could have gone.

It was a snowy night a week before Christmas when his wife called him at the school. He was working the evening shift, cleaning lockers over break to get ready for the new semester. This was going to be the best money he made all year, getting him some rare overtime.

"Jerry, there's a white thing like a cat in here." His wife sounded distressed.

"What is it, honey?"

"I mean, there's something white in here."

"Snow? It has snow on it?"

"No, like a cat, only not a cat. Short-legged."

"A dog?" Thank god it wasn't a white snake, woken up from a

winter sleep. A white snake would have been a terrifying thing for his wife to see. Not that there was any kind of white snake in the reptile book. He hoped it wasn't a dog either—he'd still been trying to convince his wife to agree to a new dog, and a strange dog showing up in the house would nix that idea.

His wife continued, breathless: "A wild thing, Jerry. Something from outside. It was in the kitchen. I slammed the door and left. Now I hear it tearing something up."

"A possum."

"Nothing like a possum. Please, Jerry, come home now."

"I'll be right there, honey." He left the mop bucket in the hallway, ran out. He almost forgot to lock the school's front door, but he returned and locked it, and then jumped in the old truck and zoomed home. When he got there, the front door was open. A winter wind blew through the house as though his wife were long gone, but she was not yet gone—she was outside loading up the minivan.

"I don't want to wake up the kids," she said when she came down the stairs. "But I can't stay here."

"Where is it?"

"What?"

"The white creature? The cat."

"I told you it wasn't a cat. A cat wouldn't have scared me. The body was long. Short legs."

"But at first you said it was like a cat."

"Forget about it being a cat."

"Where is it?"

"Outside now. I locked it in the kitchen and went around outside and opened the kitchen door and it ran out."

"What could it be?"

"I don't know. But I don't want to live with it. I don't want to live here."

"But white? What's white?"

"You're not listening to me."

"I'm listening. Of course you were scared. White and not a cat. Not snow on its fur."

"It wasn't snow. And its neck was long."

"What else is white?" Jerry said.

"It was something that wasn't supposed to be in here, Jerry. It wasn't supposed to be in a house. A house should keep something like that out. I thought with the new siding…"

Jerry wondered. Could something have come up under the siding? He wasn't a professional, after all—maybe he had made a terrible mistake installing the siding. If a white cat could get in, then there were places where that snake could enter. He hadn't secured the place at all.

He stepped into the kitchen and saw that the window above the sink was open two inches, and the new fiberglass screen was slashed roughly. Sometimes when his wife burned food, she opened the window. There was a trellis right outside; he'd installed it for roses after he'd finished with the dry well. He'd considered the flimsiness of the screens on the new windows when he'd bought them, but the window guy had assured him that nobody used metal screen anymore, that everybody used vinyl.

"It must have been a cat," Jerry said. "If it wasn't a possum, what else could it be?"

"It wasn't a cat," his wife said, tears now pouring down her face. "Smell. Does it smell like a cat? Stop saying it was a cat."

"Or maybe something albino, like an albino rabbit," he said. "Did it have red eyes?"

"It wasn't a damn rabbit."

God, she was beautiful, her skin as smooth as the skin of the girl who had broken up with him in her parents' driveway ten years ago and then jumped out of his truck and married another man. Her hair just as shiny, although she had cut it even shorter in the last few weeks, so there was no longer anything serpentine about it. Only then did Jerry realize the smell, the full smell of the thing that had been in the kitchen, rich and musky. A smell that would wake a person up once and for all.

His wife packed a bag that night and left. She came back for the kids and another load of her things the next day. That musk scent faded, but Jerry could smell it in the kitchen for weeks, and even after that he didn't forget it. And finally, he longed for the smell.

The mammal guide was a reference book, or he would have checked it out of the library. Instead he went to the nature center and bought it at the gift shop, although he should have been saving his money or paying on the credit cards. Once he got it home, he couldn't stop turning the pages, studying the moles and voles, the different types of mice and weasels. The animal in question was an ermine, no doubt, the pure white winter phase of a short-tailed weasel. He liked that phrase *winter phase*, which suggested a creature could be different season to season.

When Holroyd finally showed up again, it was an afternoon at the end of January. He looked pale, and he didn't talk about missing hunting season, so Jerry didn't bring it up. That morning, Jerry had burned shed number five to the ground, and now he was tending the embers. Holroyd backed his truck up through the snow so they could sit on the tailgate and stare into the fire and feel a little heat from it. Jerry told Holroyd about the ermine coming into the house.

"That's something, they're coming back. I never saw one. Hammermill trapped them all, trapped everything around this place. Used to sell pelts. Ladies used to love that pure white ermine fur."

"I wish I'd've seen it." Jerry thought maybe, if he'd been there, he could have helped his wife see it in a new way—a way she could have liked it. Seeing that ermine the right way could have been a nice surprise, like seeing a unicorn when you were hoping to see a deer.

"You aren't smoking?" Jerry said.

"Naw, gave it up." His fingers twitched. "Sons of bitches tell me

I'll be dead if I don't."

"I been craving a cigarette, myself, lately," Jerry said. "When I'm sitting alone."

"Don't get yourself started on that smoking again, son," Holroyd said. "Promise me."

"I won't." Jerry's eyes stung for an instant at that word, *son*.

"You ever see your snake again?" Holroyd asked.

"No, not since I was putting up the siding. Hey, you're shaking. You want to come inside?"

"Naw."

"I guess a snake like that would be hibernating now," Jerry said.

"Sure it wasn't just your imagination, playing tricks?"

"I wouldn't have something beautiful like that in my imagination. Did I tell you that up close the skin was like a prism? Showed even more colors, greens and blues."

"Shame about burning down this shed," Holroyd said. "Now there's only fifteen of 'em left. You scrapped out the wood stove, I guess." Holroyd tossed his beer can onto the embers, and they watched it blacken against the orange coals.

"My wife's getting her prefab," Jerry said. "Her parents are putting it on the lot behind their house. Nice for the kids to be near their grandparents."

"You thinking of moving in with her?"

"She hasn't asked me," Jerry said.

"Well, I'm not anyone to tell a person what to do and what not to do," Holroyd said. He splashed beer on his mustache and put the can down without managing to take a drink.

Jerry couldn't think anything bad about his wife. He didn't know why he'd started loving her in high school, why he kept on loving her, loved every move she made, every expression that showed up on her face—he just did. With her soft skin and long hair, she was a beautiful mystery, and even her fear of all the other beautiful creatures was something special about her. She had her way of living, and those kids of hers were such nice kids, and he missed them every day, but she was somebody who didn't belong here, plain and simple. It was more relaxing now, not having to worry about fixing everything up, but it didn't stop him from missing her. Jerry said, "My wife said I was always staring at her and it made her nervous. I thought it was a normal thing to look at your wife all the time."

The two men sat on the tailgate most of that Saturday afternoon. Jerry watched the old man's shaking hands, his watering eyes, and, once, a tear that ran down the side of his nose into his overgrown mustache. Anything seemed possible now that Jerry's wife was gone, any kind of sadness.

"So the old lady owns this place is still alive," Holroyd said, shaking his head in agreement with himself. "My wife watches the obits, keeps an eye out for her."

"I keep getting a paycheck. It's not much, but it's something, now that it's just me here." Jerry threw his empty can onto the fire, although it had a ten-cent deposit, and he watched it darken.

"She must be eighty, ninety years old."

"I hope she goes on awhile." Jerry wasn't thinking about the old lady, though. He was thinking about Holroyd, who was at least a decade younger than Red Hammermill, but looked almost as old, or at least today he did.

"You cut up your credit cards like you said you was going to?" Holroyd asked.

"Yup. And I got one of them payment plans like you said."

"Those cards'll drag a man down."

"I wish I could see the snake one more time," Jerry said. "Just to know it's okay."

"Maybe you ought to get yourself that dog you were talking about, now that your wife isn't stopping you. It's not good to spend too much time alone."

"I've been thinking, though. If I get a dog, I probably won't see the snake again. Not with the barking and chasing. Maybe I'll wait until I see that snake one more time in the spring."

"A lab or a retriever would make you a nice companion, better than any snake."

"I just wonder, what if he's the last of his kind?"

Holroyd handed Jerry another beer and when he popped it open, Holroyd said, "Hell, here's to the last of its kind."

Jerry supposed the last of the big orange snakes would be hiding the way any snake hid in winter, curling under the ground in his old skin. In spring, he'd poke his head up, stick out his tongue, sniff, and know he was where he belonged. Then he could get to the business of shedding and eating and seeking warmth.

World of Gas

Propane tanks reclined like rows of swollen white bellies behind the chain link, each tank emblazoned with the Pur-Gas smiling cat logo, one of the boss's idiotic conceptions—he'd apparently forgotten that the "p-u-r" was meant to be pronounced "pure." At the tire-repair shop next door, the compressors rattled and droned, and if the noise didn't actually kill brain cells, then it certainly prevented anyone in the vicinity from thinking clearly. As the Pur-Gas office manager, Susan, talked on the workroom phone, she noticed that she was wadding up her lunch bag so tightly that her knuckles were white. According to the vice principal on the other end of the phone, her oldest son, Josh, was being kicked out of school for fighting.

"Give him some kind of in-school suspension," Susan said. "Otherwise he's going to sit home watching TV all day. He should be learning something."

The vice principal said, "We don't have the personnel to monitor problem students all day."

"Well, I'm at work all day. I can't watch him."

"What about his father?"

"What *about* his father?"

"Somebody's asking for you," whispered Darcy, Susan's assistant. Darcy crossed her eyes and signaled "nutcase" by tracing a little circle in the air.

"We'll see what we can do," said the vice principal, sounding annoyed.

"Yeah, thanks a lot." Susan hung up the phone, tossed her lunch bag into the garbage can and returned to the front counter, where she found her brother-in-law Mack, dressed as usual in a camouflage jacket and army cap. For the benefit of her sister Holly and their two kids, Susan always gave Mack her employee's discount. Susan retrieved his paperwork from a file under Holly's name.

"You're sure that's the biggest one I can get?" Mack asked.

"This is a three-thousand-cubic-foot tank, Mack. It's half as big as your trailer. Try not to let any of your drunk buddies drive a truck into it." Propane was apparently the fuel of choice this month for the Y2K crowd, whose members all thought that the flow of natural gas would be compromised at the stroke of midnight December 31, 1999, along with civilization as they knew it.

Mack and his militia pals were by no means the only pain-in-the-ass alarmists in town these days. Susan had ordered survival appliances for fidgeting paper-company executives, two city council members, and, last week, the very vice principal with whom she'd just been speaking—maybe she should call him back and threaten to lose his order for the super-efficient, lightweight propane heat source if he didn't keep Josh at school. All these men thought that the big collapse was coming, and they were cocksure enough to think that through clever planning and by purchasing the right machines they would survive, huddling in their basements or manning their guard towers.

"Them delivery trucks run on propane or gasoline?" asked Mack, who was not a bad-looking guy when he wasn't done up like an idiot commando.

"Propane."

"Good. That means the trucks'll have fuel to make deliveries."

"Don't worry, the trucks'll be running."

It occurred to Susan that men were always waiting for something cataclysmic—love or war or a giant asteroid. Every man wanted to be a hot-headed Bruce Willis character, fighting against the evil foreign enemy while despising the domestic bureaucracy. Men wanted to focus on just one big thing, leaving the thousands of smaller messes for the women around them to clean up.

"You're too negative, too cynical," Susan's husband (now ex-husband) had told her. "And you don't love me the way you used to. That's why I had to find somebody else."

"Tell it to your kids," Susan had said. "Tell it to Josh and Andy and Tommy."

Men didn't understand that you couldn't let yourself be consumed with passion when there were so many people needing your attention, when there was so much work to do. Men didn't understand that there was nothing big enough to exempt you from your obligations, which began as soon as the sun rose over the paper company and ended only after you'd finished the day's chores and fell exhausted into sleep against the background noise of I-94.

This millennium business was just another distraction to keep men from being of any goddamned use whatsoever. Instead of going to all this fuss and expense, Mack ought to hire a babysitter once a week and take Holly out for dinner or maybe clean up the yard around their trailer, which, last time Susan saw it, was littered with motor-oil bottles, rotting lumber, and automobile engines covered with tarps. And now that he was preparing for Y2K, Mack had gotten hold of a 550-gallon diesel tank that lay like a big yellow turd under Holly's clotheslines. Apparently Mack was going to fill the tank with fuel for his truck.

"You've got to have a four-inch concrete pad for this propane tank," Susan said. "We're going to have to come out to inspect it before you pour, and after."

"I'm pouring the slab tomorrow." From his pocket, Mack produced some papers. With great seriousness, he said, "Susan, I know we haven't always gotten along, but you ought to have a copy of this," and he unfolded a four-page stapled packet of instructions for Y2K preparation. Susan stopped writing and read to herself randomly from the back page: "Fill your bathtub with water," and "Have a minimum of a thousand rounds of ammunition for every gun you own." The noise of the compressors next door seemed to intensify, and the men shouted and dropped tools onto the concrete floor. As usual, the radio out back was turned to the Rush Limbaugh station.

Susan looked into Mack's squinting face, wadded the pages into a ball, and tossed it over the counter, missing the can behind him by three feet. "None of you sons a bitches get it, do you?" Susan's voice grew loud. "If the power goes out, we'll all just have to live without power for a while. Whatever happens, happens. You can't control the world, and you especially can't control this propane!" Susan's voice rose to a crescendo, and Darcy looked in from around the corner, a cheese and meat sandwich falling open in her hand. Susan resumed at a whisper, "You know, if I tell the driver not to fill your tank, he won't fill it. So you'd better be good to Holly."

Mack moved away from the counter and studied his black army boots. Susan marked three places on the form where Mack had to sign and held out a pen. In a businesslike voice she said, "If you don't use a hundred dollars a month worth of this gas, you'll have to pay double rent on the tank."

That afternoon, Susan skipped swimming at the Y and went right home. Before even going into the kitchen, she followed the stairs down to the basement into which Josh, two months ago, had moved his bedroom. That had allowed Andy and Tommy to have their own rooms.

"Josh?" She tapped on the door to what used to be her husband's office, but there was no answer. She pushed the door open into a room lit only by the bluish glow of the television.

"You're home early, Mom!" Josh shouted in an accusatory tone.

"Josh, I got a call—" Susan stopped talking as soon as she realized there were two bodies in Josh's bed. "Nicole?" Josh's latest curly-haired girlfriend was with him, the sheet pulled up to her neck. As Susan's eyes adjusted, she realized Josh was naked. For Christ's sake, they were fifteen years old! Susan was struck dumb, listening, despite herself, to the intonations of surprise and anger emanating from what appeared to be *The Jerry Springer Show*. Finally, Susan yelled, "Get up!"

"I don't just come into your room," Josh said.

"Get up!" Susan stepped outside the door, crossed her arms over her chest, and tried to think of what to say. The girl came out first, with mascara smeared around her eyes. She looked at Susan defiantly before heading to the stairs; the girl's face was so pale and thin that Susan wondered if she could be one of those girls who threw up her food.

"I love her, Mom," Josh said. "You wouldn't understand that." Susan noticed that Josh's face was sprouting not just peach fuzz, but also a few wiry, dark hairs.

"Well, if you love her, then why in the hell would you take a chance on getting her pregnant?" asked Susan. "Why take a chance on screwing up both your lives?" Susan was also thinking: if this girl means so much to you, then why don't you turn off the damned TV when you're in bed with her?

Dishwashing was Susan's last chore before going to bed that night. The hot water was making her sleepy, and she let herself forget about Josh and think about Y2K. She'd been so busy scoffing at the alarmists that she hadn't let herself really think about the year 2000. She understood the principle involved with the zero-zero date and that it could cause problems with computer systems controlling traffic lights and ATM machines. Maybe she'd allow extra time to get to work on Monday, January 3. Maybe she ought to have a couple hundred dollars on hand in case her first paycheck was screwed up. She could easily fill her bathtub with water, but probably she wouldn't bother. Although her bastard of an ex-husband called her negative and cynical, she truly believed that regular people doing their jobs could fix whatever problems resulted from the glitch.

Susan opened the window to allow a stream of cold night air into the room, and she listened to the hum of traffic from the highway, the buzz of an airplane flying over, the muted din of third-shift work at the paper factory, and the sound of the TV blathering in the basement. Josh would be lying in his bed, passed out with his mouth open when she went down to turn it off. When Susan pressed the power button, he'd complain, half-asleep, "I was watching that, Mom." She knew she hadn't said the right things to him about Nicole earlier, and she was still too pissed off to know what she should say.

Susan submerged her hands in the warm water again. She could see some advantages to a real millennium breakdown. Life would be quieter without power. She imagined the hands of her kitchen clock spinning faster and faster, racing toward New Year's Eve, and then stopping. At the critical moment, she'd be standing at the sink like this, maybe burning a balsam-scented Christmas-tree candle on the windowsill. She'd be exhausted from her father's visit; he always came December 24th and stayed until New Year's Eve, which meant she had to keep the house clean all week and get up early to cook hot breakfasts for him—the man thought the world would end if they didn't all sit down to a cooked breakfast. Suddenly smoke would cease to flow from the paper-company stacks. The lights would all go out, and the factory's whirring, rattling, clanking machines would fall silent. Susan would dry her hands and put on some hand lotion and exhale deeply. In Susan's millennium moment, even the headlights of the delivery trucks would dim and die as wheels stopped turning. On all lanes of the highway, four-wheel-drive vehicles and ordinary cars would grind to a halt, along with their drivers. Overhead, the stars would shine as brightly as they did in the desert sky. Men revving motorcycles, chain saws, and lawn tractors in garages would wind down, too, their machines becoming dead, oiled metal in their hands. The voices of vice principals, men who ordered Pur-Gas, and guys jabbering on TV and radio would slow and then stop, if only for a moment. Men of all ages everywhere—men talking about football, auto engines, politics, hydraulic pumps, and the mechanics of love—would finally just shut up.

The Inventor, 1972

A rusted El Camino clips the leg of the thirteen-year-old girl, sends her flying through the predawn fog. She lands on the side of the road and lies twisted and alive in the dirty snow. Before the pain gathers its strength, the girl sees how her leg looks wrong against the asphalt. In slow time, she notices a hole in her new jeans, a puncture made when the jagged end of her broken fibula stabbed through and retracted. The El Camino backs up and parks beside her, blocking her view of the road. Beyond its low-slung bed and rusted rear bumper, she can see the pink light at the eastern horizon. *Pink sky in the morning, sailors take warning,* her father says, but this morning, the first morning she has worn her new hip-hugger bell-bottoms, she was seeing the blush of pink beyond the fog as a flower getting ready to blossom in the sky.

A car door slams. A broad-chested man in camouflage approaches, drops to one knee. His hunting license is pinned to his jacket, but the plastic sleeve is scratched and fogged, and the girl's pain has become so great so quickly, she can no longer read. On the hunter's cheek is beard stubble. Her heart pounds as he leans close, pounds harder when she sees the other side of his face, the scar, chin to temple, edged in white, a swath of flesh so raw-looking it seems as though it might melt and drip on her. She cannot back away, so she wishes momentarily to die, or at least to faint. The hunter rests a shaking hand on his knee, and she sees the flesh is similarly mottled on the back of that hand, as though the skin has liquefied and frozen.

"I didn't see you," he says in a harsh whisper. She sees a gap where a canine tooth is missing and smells sour breath. She cannot see that his throat and the alveoli of his lungs have also been seared by iron oxide and explosions of steam, but she hears his labored breathing.

A tattoo on the back of the hunter's other hand glows blood-blue. She recognizes *Comstock '56* not as letters and numbers, but as a logo, as though it is her own tattoo. She moves her lips, tries and fails to say, *Uncle Ricky*, although this man's thick outline is nothing like Uncle Ricky's. At home, on the pond-side wall of the girl's boy-blue room, *Comstock '56* is pressed in gold ink on the corner of Uncle Ricky's senior portrait. Handsome, dark-eyed, narrow-chested Uncle Ricky drowned in the pond before she was born, the month before his graduation, died in the black muck in his own homemade scuba gear. Everyone says she resembles Ricky, and this year she is parting her hair (dark like Ricky's) on the side, the way he did, rather than in the middle like the other kids at school. He has always been, for her, proof that the good die young, and this horrible man, who should have died instead of Ricky, is more proof.

"Can you talk?" The hunter spits as he speaks. The girl's stomach heaves.

She closes her eyes, presses them closed, swallows acid (notes her throat is not crushed). The pain in her leg is breathtaking; she cannot imagine uttering words, but if she had something like a walkie-talkie, she might be able to press the transmit button. Her parents should be here, saying, *Help is on the way, honey*, and *Everything will be okay*. She turns her head to one side (neck not broken) and, without opening her eyes, vomits this morning's toast and peanut butter down the side of her face.

"I'm going for help," the hunter rasps.

When he is gone, she looks down and sees blood soaking her new jeans. Her hand is bare, minus its glove. The other hand feels numb underneath her back. The girl has sometimes imagined how it would be if she died, how her family would miss her, how the two boys she likes from school, Curtis and Mark, would long for her, how beautiful she would look in her coffin. But that was yesterday or five minutes ago, before this riot of pain in her leg. Now the vision of herself in a coffin makes acid rise in her throat again. She does not want to die young. She does not want to be good like that. She presses together her thumb and middle finger, slowly—feels muscles connect, a hundred tiny levers turning, clicking into the on-position, all the way from her brain, down her arm, to her hand—and she snaps. Snaps again, because her thumb and finger still work, because her spinal cord is not severed. Snaps a third time, to snap away death. She moves her stinging hand to her face (arm bones not shattered) and wipes the vomit from her cheek.

Beside her, a slender tree trunk rises out of the snow and into the fog like a single leg. There are no songs about one-legged girls, and at school, everybody avoids the two girls in wheelchairs. Nonetheless, she realizes, one-legged would be better than dead. Her heart deflates. She has long imagined her future spreading out before her, gloriously full of love and discovery; she has been waiting for the future to arrive like a plate full of fancy appetizers in a restaurant, like a lush bunch of roses placed in her arms, like the biggest birthday cake with the brightest candles, baked and lit by people who love her.

But the snow beneath her now is not fluffy sled snow, is not pond-side drifts sculpted by wind, through which she can fly on her wooden sled out onto the ice. The snow here is metallic, sharp-edged, conductive of the pain that pulses all through her leg, radiates to her belly, her shoulder. The pain at first seemed like her enemy, but she knows now that it must not end. She clings to the pain as it blossoms, as it opens like a flower, as it grows too elaborate to be contained in this moment, so that it must swell into the future, the way a freight train blows its whistle forward to warn of its approach.

Where is the man who survived 1956, the scarred man who threw her into the air and left her in agony? Where is the man who has ruined her? The man who must get her into the future alive?

The hunter has not run in years, but he runs into the road in front of a two-tone Chevy pickup, which screeches to a halt inches from him. The hunter holds up his hand, motions for the driver to unroll his window, notices blood on his own knuckles—he has trapped and gutted three rabbits to cook for his father today. The hunter approaches the driver along the fender, clears his throat, but the driver's eyes widen and the window freezes halfway down. The driver is small-headed, with a face that resembles a rabbit's face; his knuckles, perched high on the steering wheel, have gone white. The hunter wants to explain to the driver that he has been burned at the foundry and that a girl needs help, but the driver must have seen him emerge from the fog at a certain angle that made his face look like a scary mask, because the driver guns his engine, squeals his tires, and fishtails away, without ever seeing the girl on the other side of the El Camino. His pickup spits oily carbon exhaust into the morning fog. The hunter has scared himself a few times when he's encountered unexpected mirrors. Because he has run out of his prescription ointment, the scar is burning more and tightening, tugging down the skin around his eye, making him feel as monstrous as he must look to a stranger.

He leaves his car there, thinking it will protect the girl, and runs a hundred yards around the side of the pond to the nearest house, little more than a shack. He is panting as he knocks. He knows this house, and despite the urgent situation, his heart sparks. He and Ricky Hendrickson used to smoke in the old stone garage behind this house, halfway between their own two houses; the hunter wore himself out carving his name into one stone and the word *fuck* into another, while Ricky created tiny gunpowder explosions that bit into the walls. Ricky gave him the *Comstock '56* tattoo in that garage, with India ink he'd swiped from the school's art cupboard. Ricky was the art teacher's favorite, although he drew mostly schematic diagrams of machines he planned to build someday.

After half a minute, the hunter pounds on the door of the house again with his good hand, the tattooed hand. A cold light shines from inside, but nobody answers. When he sees a plasticky curtain move, he pounds with both fists until the motion of the curtain settles. He tries the handle of the windowless door, with its thick white paint, but it is locked. He does not kick the door open, does not swing his cracked and muddy steel-toed boot into the door, but instead jogs to a house farther around the pond.

Only after much pleading does the old lady in the second house unlock the door and allow the hunter in. She wears big plastic glasses that extend above her eyebrows, the frames the blood-blue color of a tattoo, and she trains a shotgun on him the whole time, follows him with the business end from the door to the kitchen wall phone. The hunter admires her squat steadiness—the shotgun does not quaver in her hands, does not for a second relinquish its target. He fumbles, fails twice to drag his shaking finger, stuck in the zero hole, all the way around for the telephone operator.

"Please, ma'am," he rasps into the phone and tries to explain.

"I can't understand you, sir." The voice on the phone is patient, soft, a little nasal.

"Please listen," he says and closes his eyes, envisions the girl's body, the dark hair tangled around the freckled face. That face looks so familiar to him, although he knows no schoolgirls. He struggles to control his voice between breaths.

"I hit a girl on the road by the junior high. She's lying beside my car. Please send an ambulance. I didn't see her with the fog."

"Just a moment, sir," she replies. Of course, she's a telephone operator with no ambulance to command, but she promises to connect him to the ambulance dispatcher. Long seconds pass. He stares out the woman's window onto the pond, where evaporating snow rises as fog. He sees the outline of the Hendrickson house across the way and remembers the early May afternoon some kids found Ricky's body in the mud, tangled in water-lily stems. While the hunter chokes his story into the phone, the old woman does not lower her gun or offer advice that might assist him. She aims patiently as he, by himself, through careful selection and repetition of the facts, makes clear to the man on the other end what school, what road, what pond.

Footsteps like heartbeats! Someone is coming through the fog! The girl touches her thumb and middle finger together and presses. A man approaches, breathes as though he has returned from drowning, comes close, closer, leans over her the way she has wanted certain boys from school to lean close, the way girlfriends lean in to tell secrets, the way she has dreamed of Uncle Ricky coming to her in her bed. In her room, she has opened her arms and thighs to his ghost, to receive his perfect body with her perfect body, but now she smells sweat, blood, infection.

The hunter's terrible face seems the cause of her physical pain, that unbearable assurance that she is still alive, and so she will not look away. She considers another future, one without flowers or prizes or birthday cakes. What if the future were camouflage and gray and sour, phlegm and dirty snow, wounds and scars and boys killing helpless pond creatures? (She has always thought Uncle Ricky would have stopped the other boys from killing turtles and frogs.) The pink at the horizon is no longer a flower, but a ghoulish hand, with its fingers grasping upward.

"Help is on the way," the hunter says when he finally reaches her. She cannot make out his words, but his strained underwater breathing tells her something about Uncle Ricky's last breaths.

At home, in her blue room, the girl hides incense in the hole in the plaster wall where she found an ancient pack of Lucky Strikes, where she would hide love letters if she had any, where she has recently hidden her friend's copy of Xaviera Hollander's *The Happy Hooker*. The girl has been afraid to read beyond the first page because of the word *pubic*. If she lives, she will read the book. She will paint her room. White or yellow or pink. She now tries to hum the Beatles song "Eleanor Rigby," but it sticks in her throat—why, she wonders, would a face be in a jar by the door? She thinks *waterlogged*—Ricky was waterlogged. If she lives, she will move the picture of Ricky out of her room, to the stairway with the other family photos.

"The ambulance is on the way," the hunter says. "Everything will be okay."

One of his eyes seems bigger than the other, the lower lid pulled inside out to reveal red flesh like a leech's. The girl thinks the whites of his eyes are oily, ready to ignite. Any time before now, she would have turned away from this man, but this morning she has willed him to come to her.

Her freckled cheeks would be cold to the touch, the man thinks. He could press his cheek to hers, let his wound be soothed against her young skin. Some instinct tells him this girl's flesh would heal him, some ancient voice whispers that this was how men healed before doctors, before the promise of painkillers and surgeries. Surely this girl will get what surgeries she needs, but men, hunters, now as back then, must tap other sources. He could lower his face to hers, but instead he breathes deeply, knows he could not live with himself if he forced himself on her. He imagines how she would squirm to escape his burned hand pressing against her smooth naked belly. He takes off his camouflage jacket and spreads it over her legs, feels momentarily the thrill of doing the right thing, lets himself forget what he might have done. Then he hates himself for not covering her before now.

He looks into her eyes to establish how much she hates him. She meets his gaze, fixes him in her sights, but he does not see hatred. Without moving a muscle, the girl reaches out for him, grabs hold of him with her eyes. Grabs, holds, boards him like a lifeboat and clutches his gunwales. What she is doing to him with her eyes makes it even harder for him to catch his breath. He tries to look away when he hears the ambulance siren in the distance, but when he does so, her eyes seem to grip him even more securely. He has no women or girls in his life, no daughter, no little sister. He has had a few girlfriends over the years, none lately, none since burning his face. After his parents' divorce, his mother moved to Indiana, where his older sister lives.

As the girl holds him there, he silently promises her that he will not use her body and that he will save her life. But he can tell from the way she looks at him that his promise is not enough. He will dedicate himself to her, he wants to explain, although he can't give her much. He's living in his car right now, and earlier this week, to his shame, he ate half a sandwich somebody left on a table in a sub shop. He lost his tooth four months ago, yanked it himself with pliers after a year of pressure and pain, and since then two more have become infected—the blood flow is compromised on his burned side, the doctor said—so his mouth aches and tastes of metallic rot. As a result of the burns on his hand, it has been years since he shot a deer. And he's only thirty-five—other men seem so young at thirty-five.

The only happiness he has felt lately is something he can never tell anyone: the jolt of adrenalin he felt when the girl's body hit his bumper. Joy at the notion he'd hit a deer, joy that he'd have something more than rabbits to take to his father's house, joy that his father would be glad to see him. He would have carried the body out to the garage, hooked the chain around its neck and dragged the chain over a couple of rafters. He would have skinned the deer and dressed it out the way his dad had taught him.

"I didn't see you," he whispers to the girl. "I was going to visit my father." He doesn't say that he was looking through the fog toward the Hendricksons' house, as he does every time he passes, wondering who lives there now, wondering if they know what happened to Ricky.

The man and the girl share the thought that the sirens are too far away, that the ambulance technicians will never arrive. The girl sighs again, sighs like a grown-up woman who has chosen badly in marriage. The hunter sighs, too. He thinks his body was once a vessel filled with hope for the future, ideas for inventions—as a teenager, he ordered the inventor's guide out of the back of a comic book—but he long ago became a sack of broken glass. Now he has broken this girl, too, and she will never be her whole young self again.

He has always been able to clearly picture Ricky Hendrickson in his coffin, silent and pale, his freckles covered with makeup, and he has a photographic vision of Ricky building homemade bottle rockets beside the pond, with charcoal, sulfur, and saltpeter, but when he sees Ricky's face in the girl's face, he fears he is losing his mind.

"Please, don't die," he whispers.

He wonders what could be taking the ambulance so long. And he wonders why life has not delivered what it promised when he was a kid. By now cars (and ambulances!) should fly at the speed of sound as they did in the comic books. By now, he thinks, by 1972, roadside sensors should warn a driver of humans approaching the pavement, even in dark or fog, should warn an entire neighborhood of bodies submerged in ponds, of arrested breathing, of spilled blood. When a girl lies on the pavement, when a boy is drowning, everyone should run to help.

If the foundry, where he worked above vats of molten steel for sixteen years, has become obsolete, then shouldn't the world outside the foundry be noticeably more advanced? He had intended to work at the foundry forever (his burns were a pact the foundry made with him), but they disassembled and dissected the equipment with torches and sold it as scrap iron in a world unprepared to reshape those materials into advanced medical machinery. The hunter imagines not only helicopters that can rush patients to hospitals, but high-tech stainless-steel flying crafts, orbs positioned strategically throughout every community to provide relief to those in pain. He can imagine a silver globe flying toward them at bottle-rocket speed, at spacecraft speed, pausing to release a sedating gas or painkilling radio waves or calming infrared radiation. He has hurt this girl—he won't deny it—but the whole world is guilty, too, because of the achingly slow progress of technology, because of the world's refusal to soothe burns and infected teeth, to heal drowned and broken bodies. What point is there in a world like this one, he wonders, where working machinery must be melted down, where the cleverest scientists drown, where he and this girl must wait in the dirty slush alongside the road and stare into the face of pain?

The girl's freckles seem like holes through which her life might pour out—she may already be dissolving. Each of the three dead rabbits in the back of his El Camino, each flea-ridden pelt, contains about a pound of meat. After seeing the girl's wounds, he will not be able to skin the rabbits, knows, too, that they are not enough to bring his old man, who thinks his son should have more to show for his life. The siren grows louder, and the girl is still alive. He is alive with her. Tears are falling out the sides of the girl's eyes, and he feels grateful; his own tear ducts have been damaged by his not wearing goggles at the foundry.

His eyes remain locked with hers until the technicians (Modern uniformed miracles, they have arrived!) push him aside. "I didn't see her," he says in his nonsense syllables. He wonders if they sense his hunger for venison, if his hunger shows on his face. The girl sees it; he feels her watching him until they place her in the ambulance, until he hears the swoosh-swoosh-click of doors closing and latching, as securely as those on a space ship. The police ask him to get into the back of the cruiser.

He will never tell them or anyone about the outline of the girl stepping from the fog with such animal grace, her head tipped back to reveal her throat. In the next hour they will ask him repeatedly if he drove over the white line—he could have when he was looking at the Hendrickson house, although he honestly doesn't think he did. He will not tell them how the girl's face looks like Ricky's face. They will ask him if he has been drinking, and they will not believe him when he says no. The county sheriff's department has recently purchased their first Breathalyzer machine, and a second police cruiser will arrive with the machine in the trunk, and they will test him and fiddle with the adjustments and retest him repeatedly, and repeatedly he will pass. Inside his own body, however, he feels the residue of what he has drunk over the years, feels the residue of all those Friday night binges acutely, as exhaustion in his joints, in the shaking of his burned hand, in his infected jaw.

If they take him to jail, they will feed him, he thinks, and if he pleads guilty, they will sentence him, and he may be able to get his infected teeth pulled. A kindhearted jail nurse might acquire for him the ointments he is supposed to use on his burns to keep his skin elastic. If he goes to jail, though, they will impound his car. In any case, they will never let him see the girl again.

Sixteen years ago he realized he would never tell anyone that he had helped Ricky build that scuba gear out of lengths of hose he swiped from the school science lab and a welding oxygen tank nabbed from the service station. Ricky was not supposed to try the gear without him, especially not at night. After attending Ricky's funeral and looking into the coffin, the hunter had been unable to return to school, although it was only three weeks until graduation. He took the job in the Paw Paw foundry. Kids who didn't know crap said that Ricky's body had had over five hundred bloodsuckers stuck to it when they dragged him out of the muck.

The police car smells of smoke, and the hunter wishes he had a cigarette. From the back seat, he studies the face of the pond. The fog has thinned, revealing slushy ice stained pink by dawn. Nobody is skating; nobody ever skates anymore, although he recalls skating every cold day of his youth, recalls the grace of the neighborhood girls, who were mean to him in their yards, tough-talking on the road, but fluid and sweet on the ice. The hunter wonders if his old skates are somewhere at his father's house.

The girl has made him think of a time when he was fourteen, one morning between Christmas and New Year's, when he awoke before dawn. His father was working the night shift and wouldn't be home until eight a.m., so he borrowed the old man's twelve-gauge shotgun and went to the pond's edge, into the bushes in front of the Hendrickson house, where he lay on his belly and awaited the deer whose tracks he'd seen on the ice, three days in a row. Just as a pale light shone in the east, the deer emerged from the bushes, four does and a buck. They stepped across the ice, lifting their hooves high, setting each hoof down again delicately, five deer clicking like one machine whose parts were too complicated to synchronize. This would have been his first kill, and he has always felt shame at his inability to shoot the buck, but that's not what has haunted him all these years. It is more the complication of the overlapping bodies, the mystery of the herd. Their legs seemed impossibly thin on the ice, and their delicate bodies combined to become one powerful creature; they reminded him of the gangs of girls who passed him in the school hallways and at Campbell Lake in their bikinis and on the sidewalk in front of the beer store, tossing their heads, laughing.

He could have hit the buck, he is sure, if he had focused and shot right away, but he became interested in the mechanics, in whether the elaborate machine, snorting clouds of breath, would make it across the pond, whether the deer would avoid the dark patch he noticed near the bank. The hunter's head and lungs were overfilled to bursting that morning with cold, clean air, and he began to sense that the animals were, all five, going to turn and look at him in unison, or else launch into the air, into actual flight. He was warm in his snowsuit, and he remembers the way his body felt—languorous from sleep, loose-jointed, his muscles supple like that buck's. Then a shot sounded, although he had not fired, and an orange flare exploded over the ice. A second bottle rocket arced over the pond, hissing smoke, spitting sparks. At the sound, all five bodies, all twenty legs kicked out of that fussy, halting motion and leapt over the dark patch and onto the snow-covered bank, where they ran as separate beasts. Another bottle rocket flew, showering orange light above the rustle of hooves in snow.

"You bastard!" the hunter yelled. He liked the clean sound of his own voice in the cold pre-dawn air. "You son of a bitch and bastard!"

When Ricky Hendrickson shot off a fourth homemade rocket over the pond, the hunter sprang up the hill, tackled Ricky easily, rolled him over, and straddled his back. Ricky was small, didn't stand a chance against the hunter, who rubbed his face in the snow until he howled.

If only the hunter could have seen into the future. He would have gathered that skinny pest up into his arms. Would have pulled that puny freckled son of a bitch and bastard to his chest and rocked him like a girl rocked a baby doll, begged him without shame not to die. Later on, when his dad sent him to his room for getting snow in his shotgun barrel, the hunter stewed over that lost kill, imagined himself pulling the buck home around the pond on the Hendricksons' toboggan, imagined that buck already hanging in the garage when his dad got home. His dad would have spent the day in the garage with him and gone to work that night and bragged about his son, and maybe that would have changed everything. They would have eaten venison, his venison, all winter.

Back in the snow, the boys wrestled, and breath shot out wildly from their mouths and noses. The hunter shouted up at the sky, "I coulda had that buck!" Ricky shrieked and twisted as the hunter shoved snow down his back. Somehow Ricky wriggled free, tore off the hunter's wool cap, tossed it away, and said, "You couldn't hit the side of a barn, man." The hunter grabbed one insulated boot and tackled Ricky again. He reached way down the front of Ricky's jacket this time, down inside his shirt, and pressed a handful of packed snow against that kid's warm skin.

The Solutions to Brian's Problem

SOLUTION #1

Connie said she was going out to the store to buy formula and diapers. While she's gone, load up the truck with the surround-sound home-entertainment system and your excellent collection of power tools, put the baby boy in the car seat, and drive away from this home you built with your own hands. Expect that after you leave, she will break all the windows in this living room, including the big picture window, as well as the big mirror over the fireplace, which you've already replaced twice. The furnace will run and run. Then she will go to your mother's looking for you, and when she does not find you, she will curse at your mother and possibly attempt to burn your mother's house down. Connie has long admired the old three-story farmhouse for its west-facing dining room with window seats and the cupola with a view for miles around. You and Connie have discussed living there some day.

SOLUTION #2

Wait until Connie comes back from the "store," distract her with the baby, and then cut her meth with Drano, so that when she shoots it up, she dies.

SOLUTION #3

Put the baby boy to bed in his crib and sit on the living room couch until Connie comes home. Before she has a chance to lie about where she's been, grab her hair and knock her head hard into the fireplace that you built from granite blocks that came from the old chimney of the house your great-grandfather built when your family first came to this country from Finland—blocks you gathered from the old foundation in the woods. Don't look at the wedding photos on the mantle. Don't look at Connie's wide wedding-day smile, or the way her head tilts back in an ecstasy that seems to have nothing to do with drugs. Don't let the blood stop you from hitting her one final time to make sure you have cracked her skull. Put her meth and her bag of syringes and blood-smeared needles in her hand so the cops find them when they arrive. You will tell them it was an accident, that you were arguing and the argument escalated because she threatened to shoot meth into your baby.

SOLUTION #4

Just go. Head south where it's warm. After a few hours, pull over at a truck stop and call your mother to warn her to call the cops if she sees Connie. After that, pretend not to have a wife and baby boy. When put to the test, Connie might well rise to the occasion of motherhood. Contact the union about getting a job with another local. Resist taking any photographs along with you, especially the photographs of your baby at every age. Wipe your mind clear of memories, especially the memory of your wife first telling you she was pregnant and how that pregnancy and her promise to stay clean made everything seem possible. Do not remember how the two of you kept holding hands that night, how you couldn't stop reaching for each other, even in your sleep. She lost that baby, and the next one, and although you suspected the reason, you kept on trying.

SOLUTION #5

Blow your head off with the twelve-gauge you keep behind the seat of your truck. Load the shotgun with shells, put the butt against the floor, rest your chin on the barrel, and pull the trigger. Let your wife find your bloody, headless corpse in the living room; let her scrape your brain from these walls. Maybe that will shock her into straightening up her act. Let her figure out how to pay the mortgage and the power bill.

SOLUTION #6

Call a help line, talk to a counselor, explain that last week your wife stabbed you in the chest while you were sleeping, that she punches you, too, giving you black eyes that you have to explain to the guys at work. Explain that you're in danger of losing your job, your house, your baby. Tell her Connie has sold your mountain bike and some of your excellent power tools already, that you have been locking the remainder in your truck, which you park a few blocks away from the house now. Try to be patient when the counselor seems awkward in her responses, when she inadvertently expresses surprise at the nature of your distress, especially when you admit that Connie's only five foot three. Expect the counselor to be even less supportive when you say, hell yes, you hit her back. Tell the counselor that it's the little things, too, that at least once a week Connie rearranges things in the house, not only the furniture, but your financial files and the food, all of which last week she moved to the basement, including the milk and meat, which you then had to throw away. Then realize that the counselor probably has caller ID. Hope that the counselor doesn't call Social Services, because a baby needs his momma. Assure the counselor that Connie is a good momma, that she's good with the baby, that the baby is in no danger.

SOLUTION #7

Make dinner for yourself and your wife with the hamburger in the fridge. Sloppy joes, maybe, or goulash with the stewed tomatoes your mother canned, your mother who, like the rest of your family, thinks your wife is just moody. You haven't told them the truth, because it's too much to explain, and it's too much to explain that, yes, you knew she had this history when you married her, when she got pregnant, but you thought you could kick it together, you thought that love could mend all broken things—wasn't that the whole business of love? Mix up some bottles of formula for later tonight, when you will be sitting in the living room feeding the baby, watching the door of the bathroom, behind which your wife will be searching for a place in her vein that has not hardened or collapsed. When she finally comes out, brush her hair back from her face, and try to get her to eat something.

The Burn

After ten at night you had to prepay for gas at the station in Plainwell, and Jim Lobretto didn't realize how much his empty two-gallon can stank of fuel until he got it inside. He might have left the can outside the door while he paid, but knowing his luck, some bastard would steal it. He warmed his hands by rubbing them together and got himself a foam cup for coffee. Because he'd met the girl at the bowling alley bar, he'd spent more money than he'd intended, and because he'd given her a ride home, all the way out to hell-and-back Orangeville, he'd run out of gas two blocks shy of here. He had only seven dollars left: three for gas, three for cigarettes, and one for coffee to keep him awake on the drive back to Kalamazoo.

At first Jim Lobretto thought he'd wait for the fresh pot of coffee somebody had just started, but the machine dribbled with an aching slowness beside the fluorescent-lit single-serving bags of chips and the stale doughnuts under scratched Plexiglas. He'd been awake nearly twenty-four hours already, and he apparently wasn't young enough for this anymore. Jim picked up the old pot of coffee. As he poured the burnt contents into his cup, a big Ford pulled up in front of the glass wall of the gas station, a spanking new red F-250. Didn't even have plates yet, just a dealer paper taped to the window. Lucky son of a bitch.

"Shit!" Jim howled as the coffee overflowed onto his hand. He dropped the cup and it exploded like a liquid bomb, splashing the cupboard and his legs. Coffee spread on the floor around him, making him feel as though he'd wet his pants. A few drops stained the pale leather shoes of a young woman holding a gallon of milk. She looked at him through her oval glasses as though he were a dog turd and turned away before he could apologize. He picked up the cracked white cup and tossed it into the garbage. He wiped his hands on his pants, scraping his burned thumb and finger.

The woman behind the counter sighed. "Don't worry about that spill, sir. I'll take care of it."

If his car hadn't run out of gas two blocks away, if he weren't out of cigarettes, he might have walked out, might have let the door slam shut and separate him from the whole lousy business. Instead, he stood there watching as a small, ferrety-looking guy slipped out of the driver's seat of the new Ford and weaseled up to the counter in front of him. Jim could tell that everything was going that guy's way. He probably had some union job that paid twice as much as Jim's job at the foundry. And now he was driving around showing off his truck, day and night, probably hoping for snow so he could use his four-wheel drive. Jim would have liked to tell the guy it was too damned cold for snow, so he ought to just calm down. When the guy left, Jim moved toward the counter, said he wanted two gallons of gas and a hard pack of Marlboros.

"And I'll pay for that coffee."

"You don't got to pay for it," the woman said. She was fat and pink like his dad's new wife.

"I said I want to pay for it." His words hung in the air, sounded like a threat, even to him. He reminded himself that this lady worked by the hour and was going to have to clean up the coffee whether he paid for it or not. While Jim waited for his few pennies change, he wondered if the woman had children who demanded bigger allowances from her. Maybe she had a husband or a boyfriend who was always on her about being fat. He didn't want to waste his time thinking about strangers, but he'd gotten his head all loosened up from talking to that girl tonight. She said she was going back to get her nursing degree at the community college where his dad's new wife worked.

Jim had been in the doghouse with his old man since a few weeks after the courthouse wedding. He'd been having some beers with his dad, and he'd said something. It was something he and the guys at work said about fat women, and he'd been thinking the thought since first laying eyes on the new wife. Halfway through saying it, Jim changed his mind and wanted to stop himself, but the whole thing came out anyway. "How do you screw her?" he'd asked. "Roll her in flour and look for the wet spot?" His dad had turned away, disgusted. Although the old man himself used to make jokes like that, Jim knew it had to be different when you had a fat woman of your own.

The new Ford truck headed off toward the highway, and Jim carried his can of gas the two blocks back to his old Barracuda. He'd had plans about fixing up the car in his old man's garage, but now the wife's car was in there. At Jim's apartment in Kalamazoo, he had only on-street parking, because the lesbians upstairs had made a deal with the landlord to use the whole garage. By the end of this winter, if Jim didn't do something, his rear body panels would be rusting through.

When he thought all the gas was out of the can, he yanked out the plastic spout, and about a cup of fuel splashed down his right leg, all over his thigh and knee, colder than ice water. "Son of a bitch!" he yelled into the empty street. "Son of a bitch!" he repeated. A light came on in the second-floor window above a grocery with a Mexican sign. Jim briefly regretted shouting, but he figured the Mexican guy was in a warm bed and was going back to sleep, while Jim had to drive fifteen miles home. When he noticed a Virgin Mary in a bathtub in the tiny front yard of the store, he made the sign of the cross as an automatic gesture and then felt stupid and hoped nobody had seen. Maybe a guy up there in the apartment had insomnia and had finally gotten to sleep for the first time in a week. Or maybe Jim's shouting had made their baby cry, so the guy's wife had picked up the baby and was feeding it from a swelled-up breast. Anyhow, Jim told himself, he didn't give a crap.

As the heater kicked on, the inside of his car began to stink of gasoline, and he unrolled the window about four inches to cut the smell. He rolled the window back up when he started to freeze.

Just before he turned onto the highway, a sign flashed, "$39.99 single," advertising tiny cabins. If he'd had the money, he might have stopped. Nothing was waiting for him at home other than an unmade bed and a plant that had been there when he moved in. And the dykes upstairs who held hands whenever they headed out to the garage. They rode double on a Harley Sportster 1200, which meant Jim Lobretto couldn't get a motorcycle so long as he lived there, because he couldn't afford a decent one that big, and he definitely couldn't afford a Harley. The women must have put their bed right up against the heating duct, because he sometimes heard them moaning. He got mad at them for intruding on him with their pleasure, but he always listened, and all those sounds made him worry that a man might never make a woman feel as good as another woman could. He'd never mentioned the lesbians to the guys at work, although they'd have enjoyed the hell out of the situation. He didn't want them coming over trying to hear the sounds.

Jim himself hadn't had much luck with women, unless you counted bad luck. He'd thought things were improving tonight. Before heading home after a wasted visit with his dad, he stopped at Plainwell Lanes, where he met a girl and bought her three wine coolers. She had a round, pretty face, a clear complexion that made him think she'd just rinsed and patted her face dry with a clean towel. She said she lived outside of town and her friend had gone off with a guy, and so Jim offered her a ride. Twenty miles later, twenty miles farther away from Kalamazoo, it turned out she was living with her mom and dad in order to go back to school, and she kissed Jim goodnight lightly on the lips, as though he were some fucking prom date. It was a kiss-off, for sure.

The stink of gasoline helped Jim stay awake all the way to the first Kalamazoo exit. He was running on autopilot when he turned off the highway and when he continued through the intersection where they'd installed a new stoplight a few months ago. When the light turned red, he did not ease to a stop. He was almost home, and he did not want to sit and rot waiting beside the stinking paper mill for the light to turn green—hell, some black guys could jump out from under the bridge and rob you while you were waiting on that damn light. As Jim cruised through the intersection, red and blue lights flashed, as though the son-of-a-bitching cop had been sitting there all night just waiting for him.

Jim pulled to the side of the road and fastened his seatbelt in hopes the cop wouldn't notice he hadn't been wearing it, and he waited. Cops didn't hurry—they sat back there running your plates for five or ten minutes, searching for a bench warrant or some shit. Cops got paid for being out there, and they didn't care if you had other places to get to. If the cop searched his car, he'd find his dad's shotgun in the trunk, but there was no law against that. Jim pulled out a cigarette and a packet of matches from Plainwell Lanes. A few years ago, wasting a Friday night at a bar with a girl was fun, but tonight the whole thing made him feel old. The guys at work used to go to bars with him, but now they sat home with their wives and girlfriends.

He held the book of matches up to the window to read them by the streetlight: a silhouette of three bowling pins on the front, and the girl's phone number inside beneath her name, *Stephie*. He hadn't realized she'd given him her phone number. She must've stuck it in his pocket when she kissed him. That was something, anyway; the girl wanted Jim to call her. When he struck the first match, most of the burning tip flew off, and what was left went out.

"Cheap-ass matches," he said. He struck another and lit the cigarette. When his leg first began to burn, it felt merely like a confirmation that he had successfully lit his cigarette. It took a few seconds for him to feel the heat on his leg. With the cop's lights blaring through his back window, he couldn't make out exactly what was burning him. When the heat increased, he flinched and the cigarette between his lips fell into his lap and down between his legs. He pulled at his crotch to retrieve it, and only then registered the blue glow on his right leg. He slapped his thigh under the steering wheel in a failed attempt to snuff out the flame.

Finally, he unlatched the door handle, intending to jump out, but the cop, a short-haired white man who seemed eight foot tall, was standing there with a gun on him. He said, "Remain in the car."

"Holy fuck," Jim said.

"Don't move. Don't do anything stupid." The cop seemed nervous. This was how people got shot, Jim knew, by making cops nervous, but he couldn't help himself.

"Sir! My leg is on fire."

"Open the door slowly." The cop stepped back.

"You don't understand," Jim said. As he opened the door all the way, the flame on his leg turned from translucent blue to live orange. The vinyl on the steering wheel began to smolder and stink.

The cop stepped back. "Get out and roll. And keep your hands where I can see them."

"Yes sir." Jim wore his seatbelt so rarely that in his panic he tugged against the belt and grunted without even trying to unhook it.

"Get out of the car, man," the cop said. "Hurry up. You're burning. I can smell your damn flesh burning."

Jim grabbed at the wrong side of his seat a few times before remembering where the latch was and unfastening it. He held up his hands and let himself fall onto the pavement, hoping to meet ice or snow to help put out the flame, but the road was clean and dry. He rolled onto his stomach and onto his back and pressed and patted his hands over the hole burned in his jeans, but still felt like he was on fire.

"You wouldn't have been destroying evidence, would you?" said the cop, his gun still pointed at Jim.

"My leg, my hands," Jim groaned. Already burned once from

the coffee, his right hand now screamed as though the skin would slide off. "I'm burning up."

"I'll call a medic." The cop backed slowly to his car, his gun still trained on Jim. The creases stood out on the cop's pants, front and back. Probably some woman ironed them for him, probably some woman really loved this mean cop bastard.

In the ambulance, EMTs cut away one leg of what was Jim's newest pair of Levis. Twenty-eight fucking dollars down the drain. Not that he could ever have worn them with the right thigh burned off, but on the way to the hospital, he focused on that loss instead of on his leg.

"We're giving you something for the pain now," said the emergency room doctor, who spoke with an accent. Maybe he was an Indian from India or one of those island countries. Jim searched for a name for what the man was, but he couldn't come up with one. *Dagos* were Italians, weren't they? *Camel jockeys* were guys from the Middle East. The guys at work would have had something to call this guy to put him in his place.

Within about twenty minutes of somebody shoving an IV line into the back of Jim's wrist, his leg was feeling better, his hand soothed. Within the hour he was feeling relaxed, more relaxed than he had felt in a while. The next person attending him was a dark-eyed woman with a wide face; as she worked over him, he gazed into her eyes, and he felt almost good, thinking that a girl had kissed him and given him her phone number. When he next awoke, someone was bandaging his leg, and he heard a voice, which at first seemed soft, until it registered to Jim that it was a man's voice.

"Good, you're awake," the man said. "I'm George. How are you feeling?"

"Like shit," Jim said.

"I believe you."

"I need a cigarette."

"We can get you a patch."

"I don't want a damned patch. A patch is not the same as a cigarette."

"You've been burned badly, Mr. Lobretto."

"You're not going to take skin off my ass, are you?"

"You may need skin grafts," he said. "First you'll need hydrotherapy."

"What's 'hydrotherapy'?" Collecting each thought was a struggle against the medication.

"Hydrotherapy involves the application of medicated water, baths or showers. You'll come to the burn center for daily treatments."

"You want me to take a bath up here every day?"

"Mr. Lobretto, a burn like this can get infected, can even result in your losing the leg if you don't take care of it."

"How much is all this going to cost?"

"You can talk to the case worker about that."

"I didn't ask for charity," he said. "I've got insurance. And you aren't taking the skin off my ass."

"We don't have to decide on treatment right this minute."

"I want to go home." The comfort he felt at the notion of *home* had no relation to his apartment. Maybe he could stay at his dad's house for a few days. Except that his dad probably wanted to be alone with his new wife. Probably they made love all the time, wrassling around together, all balled up roly-poly.

"You should watch me change your bandages so that you'll be able to do it yourself when you do go home."

"Why do I got to have a fucking male nurse? Where's the woman who was here?"

"I'm a physician assistant, a burn specialist." The hospital lights blazed, and the man looked clean, as clean as a priest, naked in his cleanness. Jim's face hadn't been scrubbed like the PA's since he was a boy and somebody else had washed him (an aunt maybe, his mother's sister?) before going to church. A guy like this couldn't possibly understand a man like Jim who poured molten metal, a guy who operated slow-moving mechanical arms that dipped red-hot iron into etching vats. This guy was probably a fag, a friend of the lesbians upstairs from his apartment.

"I want to get out of here," Jim said.

"We'd like you to stay in the hospital for twenty-four hours."

"You can't make me stay." Jim didn't know why he wanted to leave, maybe because this guy wanted him to stay. Maybe because he wanted a cigarette.

"That's right, we can't. But you'll have to sign a paper saying you're leaving against our advisement. You're at risk of infection if you don't come back, and you're going to be in pain. The morphine is blocking you from feeling the full extent of it right now."

"Can't you give me medication to take at home?"

"I can give you the first pill, and then you'll have to fill a prescription. It won't feel like this though. With the Vicodin you're going to know you're in pain." The PA dressed the wound while Jim watched, but the morphine was making it difficult to feel the connection between the leg and himself. When he gazed directly at the wound, it seemed as if he were looking into a big wet torn-up eye.

The PA wrote on his chart and asked, "By any chance, do you want to see a priest?"

"Why the hell would I want to see a priest?"

"Your chart says you're Catholic," the man said. "It says you were born here in this hospital."

"I don't need a priest."

"I'll put some salve in a little tub for you to take home," the man said. "But like I showed you, you should never touch the open wound, just salve the skin around it to keep it from tightening up. I'll need to see this burn in forty-eight hours. I'll give you a paper that describes what you need to do and contains information about hydrotherapy."

Jim Lobretto thought the medical system was designed to make you feel dumb and helpless. And if he hadn't had insurance, this burn fag nurse and all the rest of them wouldn't be trying so hard to keep him here.

"You can't keep me here against my will," Jim muttered, forgetting and then remembering he'd already established that he was leaving.

"No, we can't."

Jim signed papers and accepted the appointment card for treatment at nine a.m. Monday, and noticed the PA gave him a prescription for only two days' worth of Vicodin. Jim listened as best he could to the directions about changing the bandage once a day. If the guys from work were here, he would have made some kind of joke about the situation. He had earned a reputation with them for being tough by resetting his own broken finger on the work floor a few years ago; Jim had been so freaked out at seeing the way his finger was bent that he yanked the thing straight without thinking. His boss had driven him to the hospital, and he'd never let on how scared he was. With those guys you had to have something that was especially tough about you, and Jim had never been in jail or the marines like the rest of them.

He limped to the lobby of the hospital and was startled by a fountain of the Blessed Mother, gazing toward heaven, her arms outstretched. He reached out and dipped his burned hands in that fountain to cool them, but pulled them out when he saw the receptionist watching him.

The sun had already risen. As he limped, stiff-legged, a half mile to where his car still sat on the shoulder of the road, discomfort gradually gave way to something much worse. He found under his windshield wiper a twenty-dollar parking ticket and threw it into the back seat. Despite the cold, Jim Lobretto was sweating. He got into his car by stretching his right leg into the passenger seat area, and he drove by operating both pedals with his left foot. Arranging his leg that way hurt enough that he took the single pill the doctor had given him. Traffic was light early on a Saturday morning, and nobody noticed when he ran a stop sign by accident. His car stank of burned vinyl and plastic from the scorched steering wheel. Smoke had darkened the windshield above the driver's side. Although the PA had said his hand didn't need wrapping, it stung as he clutched the wheel.

Once home, he positioned himself carefully on the couch in his first-floor apartment, and the combination of the pill and what was left of the morphine gave him a few hours during which the pain was bearable, but gradually his knee and thigh began to burn as though still on fire. He limped into the kitchen, reached up over the sink and found an unopened pint of Jack Daniels. He drank the whole thing and passed out.

He awoke on his back, throat parched, with the bright sunlight drying him. Heat rose through the bandage on his leg, rose from inside his body, and he wondered if maybe the doctors hadn't been able to put out the flame, which was still melting the flesh, radiating heat out from the bone.

The light meant it must be afternoon. He managed to limp to the sink by hopping on one foot, holding the burned leg stiff. He drank a pint jar of tap water, paused to catch his breath, and drank another pint, more water than he'd drunk in a long time. Outside the kitchen window were four different kinds of bird feeders hanging in the trees above the complicated birdbath fountain the lesbians had put out there, with the little stream running down into a pool and the word *peace* written on the side. A few times when he was drunk he'd considered going out there and pissing into it, but now that trickle of water suggested a promise of comfort—*hydrotherapy*. The whiskey had been a mistake, he now knew. He wouldn't drink any more whiskey—he'd drink beer instead. Beer would keep him hydrated, like *hydrotherapy*. He took a cigarette out of the pack on the counter, but there were no matches within his reach, and he couldn't imagine turning on the gas burner and leaning close to the flame.

He went into the living room, where he sat on the couch near the heating duct and slowly unwound the bandage from mid-thigh to knee and pulled up the gauze. What he saw made him sick. He replaced that same gauze and wrapped it back up without putting the salve around the edge. Then he wondered if he'd wound the bandage too tightly, because his leg ached and burned worse than before.

Jim kept planning to go out to the pharmacy and get the Vicodin and to use the pay phone to call his dad, but his body was sluggish. Then it got to be night, and he realized the pharmacy would be closed, which meant he'd have to suffer until Sunday noon. The closest thing he could find in his cupboard to painkillers were some over-the-counter sleeping pills, so he took four and lay in a dull, nightmarish stupor in his bed. Although the pain didn't let up, time eventually did pass in the cool darkness, and he kept thinking back to the wound he'd glimpsed only for a second. The puffy edges and the wet, raw center had made him think of women's eyes when they cried.

As he lay there, he heard whispers filtering down from upstairs, and he thought a woman's voice said, "Jimmy Jim-Bo," as his mother used to call him when he was tiny. His father said those memories were his imagination, that he couldn't have remembered his ma, who left when he was three and died two years later, but he was sure he knew her voice. He got out of bed and limped back to the couch, nearer the heating duct so he could hear the women upstairs. When Jim had first moved in, he had invited the women to share some barbecued sausages with him, and the bigger one had told him they didn't eat meat. Once, though, he had given the smaller gal a beer, and she had accepted it and stood with him drinking it in the backyard, beside the birdbath fountain.

Jim stared up at the ceiling panels. He wished there were cool breezes in his apartment, birds flying around and creating currents with their wings. He wished he were surrounded by soft material that barely touched him, bandages made out of silk or flower petals. That girl had kissed his lips so lightly outside her house, and she had tasted sweet, like fruit or flowers. He could call her number and explain what had happened, and she would say that the pain must be unbearable, and he'd say it wasn't that bad. He found his hacked-off jeans on the floor and searched the pockets for those matches, but the pockets were empty—the stuff must be in that plastic bag they'd handed him at the hospital. He was pretty sure he'd carried the bag to his car. Or maybe the matches had burned up or fallen onto the road with him. Outside, the sun was rising, making the gauzy clouds appear pink like rare-cooked meat.

When someone knocked at the door, his clock said 10:30 a.m. It was a miracle, he thought, the women upstairs had come to help him. Standing up made his leg erupt with heat, and his eyes watered. He stood still for a moment to let the pain subside, but it didn't subside. Maybe the women would bring him food or get his medication for him. He limped to the door and opened it to find two black women in long skirts and winter coats, with their shoulder-length hair neatly formed into white-lady hairdos. They were turning away, but when he opened the door, they turned back to him, and he felt a great disappointment that they were strangers and that they were black.

"We'd like to talk to you about the word of the Lord," said the first woman gently and glanced at the other woman for reassurance. They both stared at his leg. Then Jim remembered that he was clad only in boxer shorts. He saw that yellow fluid had seeped through his bandages.

"It's not piss," he said. "I've been burned. Badly burned." A few tears fell from his eyes, in relief at telling someone.

"We'll come back another time," said the second woman, who was younger.

"No," Jim said. It was black men who scared him, he realized, not black women. He had never known black women. Or black men for that matter. He said, "Please, come in."

"You're hurt," the first woman said. Jim could tell she was kind-hearted.

"I'm burning up." He had to wipe his eyes.

"We'd better go," said the other woman. She pulled at the arm of the kindhearted woman.

"The Lord will heal," the kindhearted woman said. She stepped closer to Jim. Her heart-shaped face glowed, and Jim got the idea that if she would put her hands on his burn, it might heal. Along with the rest of the guys at work, he had sometimes used the word *nigger*. The tinge of regret he'd felt each time now turned to acid in his belly. Now these women were the only ones who could help him.

"Can you forgive me?" Jim said. He looked into the woman's eyes.

"Ask God to forgive you." The woman smiled and reached toward him, but the other woman tugged her by the wrist and pulled her away. Jim Lobretto grabbed at the kind woman's other hand, but he managed to touch only her fingertips, and she slipped easily from his grasp. Her wedding ring told Jim that she loved some man, healed some man, but she would not heal him. The two women moved out of the doorway and along the sidewalk toward a four-door car sitting there with the motor running.

"You bitch," he mumbled. "She was going to help me. She could have." Jim Lobretto stepped outside to watch the women go. The women glanced back only after they reached the safety of their car. Two black men sat in the front seat, wearing suits. Jim wondered if the men might get out and beat the hell out of him. His hand still tingled where he had touched the woman's fingers.

When he went back inside, hurt rose like flames out of every corner of his apartment, from the sink, from the dried-out plant Jim had never once watered. Every edge of every piece of furniture threatened him. The voices on the TV were sharp. The pain of that broken finger at the foundry had been nothing compared to this; he'd break all ten of his fingers to be released from this hell. The heat from the burn had reached his throat; the acid from inside his body had reached his eyes, which now felt hot and dry. He drank another pint of water standing over the sink, staring into the backyard. Even in the cold, the birdbath fountain didn't freeze. At the top were some ceramic flowers and two birds sculpted in concrete.

"Stupid dykes," he whispered to himself and felt the acid of the word *dyke* burn his face. He didn't want to use that word again, not even with the guys at work.

The women were making the floor creak beside their bed, so he returned to the couch. He had never treated them badly, he told himself. He had helped the small woman with her car once when she needed a jump. And by not telling the guys at work about them, he had protected them. He heard the women fall together onto the bed. He didn't turn up the TV volume to drown out their breathing as he might have, but leaned against the ductwork and listened as whispers gradually turned to quiet gasps, which grew louder to become drawn-out moans. He imagined their soft bodies, their bare feet, their cool, meaty lips. The big one had long, shiny hair, which must frame her face on the bed, must spread out from her face like rays of light. Jim thought of the girl from the bowling alley lying on a soft bed, inviting him in a whisper to lie at her side. If he could find the phone number, he could shave and put some of that oil on his hair to make it lie flat, and he'd drive to her house.

"Oh, God," moaned one of the women upstairs. As Jim listened, he let his forearm fall across his leg, and the pain of the burn erupted anew. How had he been so stupid as to move his body that way?

"Oh, oh, oh, oh!" one of the women gasped. And then the voice broke free: "Sweet Jesus, yes! Oh, yes! Yes!"

"Shut up!" Jim screamed into the heating duct. "Stop doing that!" His heart raced, and he stood too quickly, and the bandage pulled, and then he banged the leg against the arm of the couch and collapsed. He sat there feeling his whole existence reduced to hot throbbing. Silence ensued and then whispers and then silence again. Whatever he used to have with those women before yelling at them, it was gone, and he already missed it terribly. Now he really was alone, at the mercy of the burn that would continue to devour him, continue to sear through tendons and muscles; even his bones would disappear, become a little pile of ashes, as though he had never existed. He needed some sort of special water, blessed water. Mary Magdalene had mopped Christ's brow with a cool, wet cloth, but Jim had never realized the importance of that gesture, had never known it was *hydrotherapy* for Christ's burning soul. Christ had become small like a child in her arms as she soothed him.

He needed that girl's phone number badly enough that he stepped out his front door into the cold and made his way to his car, which was parked out from the curb, almost far enough out to disrupt traffic. Stephie, who was studying to be a nurse, whose voice on the phone could soothe him. The matches were nowhere in the front or back seats. He opened the trunk and found the gas can and his father's shotgun lying on top of an army blanket. Jim would clean the gun for his father before he returned it. He would call his old man and ask if he could stay at his house while he healed. He lifted the shotgun out and held it to his chest, and when he looked up at the second-story front window, he saw the women watching him from between lavender-patterned curtains. Their faces seemed longer and thinner than he remembered, and their mouths formed *o*'s. He gripped the shotgun more tightly and shook his head no, meaning, no, this wasn't his gun, and he wasn't going to do anything with it except clean it, but the women's faces receded from the window.

When he returned to his front door, he discovered it had locked behind him. He grasped at his pockets for a key, but he was wearing only boxer shorts. He limped around to the back of the house, to the fountain. Somehow the birdbath fountain resembled the girl from the bowling alley. There was no end to the life inside the birdbath or inside the girl, for her blood and fluids kept flowing and flowing. Above him, at the top of the back stairs, the two women stood wrapped in their winter coats. The smaller woman had her hand on the doorknob, as though unsure whether to stay or go back inside.

"Bastards," he said aloud to the guys at work, the ones who would call him *nigger-lover* and *dyke-lover*. They all had their wives and their girlfriends at home, so they had nothing to say about him. No matter how they talked at work, Jim knew they got down on their hands and knees for those women every night. Those guys he worked with got saved every night when they went home.

The smaller woman opened the door to go back inside, but froze when Jim spoke.

"I need this water," Jim shouted. His bandages were soaked through with fluid the color of piss, and he realized that all the water and whiskey he'd been drinking must have flowed through him, must have wept right out of that wounded eye in his leg. He dipped his hands in the fountain and sloshed water over the side. He dropped the shotgun and tore off his bandage, revealed the raw meat of his leg to the cold air, to the holy water, to the women. He shouted to them, "I'm burning. The doctors couldn't put out the fire."

"I think he really needs help," said the smaller woman. A fluffy white cat slipped out the open door and stood beside the two women, its tail defying gravity.

"You can douse the flame," Jim said.

The big woman's shiny hair gleamed in the cold sunlight. She stood silent, her hooded parka almost the same color as the sky, her arms crossed over her chest, studying him. She was nearly as big as his father's wife, but she seemed as light as bird feathers up there.

The small woman said, "Should we call an ambulance? And what the hell's up with that gun?"

When he realized he was once again holding the shotgun to his chest, he tossed it away with enough force that he fell onto his ass in the snow.

The big woman said nothing, but uncrossed her arms. When she began to descend the stairs, Jim closed his eyes and prayed.

Family Reunion

"No more hunting," Marylou's daddy rumbles. Mr. Strong is a small man, hardly bigger than Marylou herself, but he's got a big voice, and some people call him just *Strong*, without the *Mister*. "We got more than enough meat. You understand what I'm saying, child?" He stands up from the stump where he's been sitting, sharpening the butcher knife, and glances around, looking for her, and Marylou fears he will also spot the yellow paper stapled to the beech tree. Marylou has just noticed the paper herself, and she is sneaking around the side of the house, intending to jump up and yank it down before he sees it, but she is not quick enough. He puts down the butcher knife and whetstone and moves to the tree.

Strong is freshly shaven for work—the new job makes him go in on Saturdays—and Marylou can see his jaw muscles grinding as he reads. Under his green wool cap, his forehead veins are probably starting to bulge. She didn't notice anybody putting up the invitation, but maybe one of her cousins snuck over here after dark last night. Uncle Cal couldn't have posted it himself, because of his tether and the restraining order, in place on account of the trouble at last year's Thanksgiving reunion party. Ever since Grandpa Murray died, though, Cal has been the head of the Murray family (not to mention president of Murray Metal Fabricators, the only shop in town paying a decent wage), and so in Strong's eyes, the photocopied invitation has come straight from Cal.

Marylou and Strong have just finished stringing up a six-point buck, Marylou's third kill of the season and two more than the legal limit. When Strong found her dragging the body toward the house an hour ago, he reminded her that being only fourteen didn't make her exempt from the law. Some day she would like to try hunting with the new Marlin rifle she won in the 4-H competition, but they live below Michigan's shotgun line, and, anyway, she knows a .22 bullet can travel a mile and a half, far enough that you might hit somebody you never even saw. Not that Marylou has ever missed what she was aiming for. She took this third buck in the woods at dawn, and the single shotgun blast echoed along the river and awakened Strong. He used to get out of bed early, but nowadays he usually stays up late and sleeps until there's barely enough time to shave and get to work.

But Strong seems to have forgotten about getting to work now. He shakes his head and says, "Son of a bitch." All he needs to see are the words *Thanksgiving Pig Roast*, and he knows the rest, that it's the famous yearly family gathering of the Murrays, when uncles and aunts and truckloads of cousins come in from out of town, and even outside of Michigan, to play horseshoes and drink beer and eat pork. Worst of all, the paper is stapled too high for Strong to reach up and tear it down.

He storms off and returns a few minutes later with his chainsaw and yanks the starter until the motor roars. He jabs the tip of the saw into the beech, knee-high. Sawdust flies, and with one clean, angry slice, the adolescent tree is free of its roots.

As the beech falls, Marylou notices the few marks where she and Strong carved dates and lines for her height in the smooth bark. The tree is taller than she has realized, and the top hangs up on a big swamp oak before breaking free by taking down one oak arm with it. When the beech lands between Strong's truck and the venison-processing table, it smashes a honeysuckle bush. Strong puts his foot on the downed trunk and cuts some stove-length pieces. When he reaches the invitation, he shreds it with the chain.

"Nerve of that bastard." His white breath mingles with the oily blue smoke.

When he notices Marylou staring at his face he says, "You got something to say, child, say it."

Marylou looks away from him, across the river, toward the Murray farm, toward the white house and the two red barns. The big wooden barn would be full of hay this time of year, and she knows how the cold morning sun streams through the cracks inside, the shafts of sunlight full of hay dust. Behind that barn is the hill where she used to shoot targets with Uncle Cal and her cousins, before all the trouble.

She decided to stop talking last year because she discovered that she could focus more clearly without words, and by concentrating hard with her breathing, she has gradually learned to slow time by lengthening seconds, one after another. In target or skeet shooting, she sometimes used to fire without thinking, but on opening day this year, she took her first careful, deliberate aim at a living thing. As she set her sights on that buck, she found she had all the time in the world to aim—up from the hooves and legs or else down from the head and neck, smack in the chest, touch the trigger, and *bang*.

On the way to his truck, Strong is shaking his head in exasperation, and once he's inside, he slams the door hard. When he pulls away, the truck's back wheels dig into the ice crust of the two-track. Marylou hears him throw up gravel on the road, and she hears the truck's noisy exhaust as it crosses the bridge downstream. No, she doesn't have anything to say, yet. And it was not just out of loyalty to the Murrays that she wouldn't open her mouth for a trial last year—her daddy is wrong there. At the time she didn't have things figured out, and even now she is still puzzling through what really happened.

This morning she puzzles about the invitation on the tree. It certainly wasn't meant for her mother, Cal's sister—she ran off to Florida with a truck driver and only calls home a few times a year. And it definitely wasn't meant for Strong—although he worked for the Murrays for years, they've never liked him. *The man broods*, Uncle Cal has always complained. Even Anna Murray used to say, *Loulou, don't brood like your father*. Marylou tried to defend him, but the Murrays could not understand that a person sometimes needed quiet in order to think about things.

The invitation on the tree has to mean that, despite all the trouble, the Murrays want to keep Marylou in the family, and Marylou feels glad to be wanted by them, by Anna who taught her to cook, and by Cal who taught her to shoot. And having boy cousins has been as good as having brothers.

Marylou kicks at the lengths of wood Strong has cut. The beech is too green to burn or even split this year. She retrieves the sharpened knife from the stump and returns to her strung-up buck. She wants to hurry and get the first long cut behind her. She will be fine after that, once the guts slosh into the galvanized trough, but she hates that first slice that turns the deer from a creature into meat. Strong would do it if she asked, but Grandpa Murray always told her, from the time she was little, how important it was to do a thing herself. She reaches up and inserts the knife about a half inch, just below the sternum. Pulling down hard and steady on the back of the blade with her free hand, she unzips the buck from chest to balls, tears through skin and flesh, and then closes her eyes for a moment to recover.

A gunshot yips from the Murray farm across the river, and Marylou drops her knife into the tub of steaming entrails. A second shot follows. Uncle Cal's black Lab begins to bark. Marylou has known this day would come, that Strong would one day kill her uncle with the pistol he carries behind the seat of his truck. And now Strong will go to jail, and she will have to move to Florida to live with her mother. Two more shots echo over the water.

Marylou considers the hole she has dug for the deer guts, and she knows she has to act fast to cover up her daddy's crime. She will bury Cal. Except she'll have to get the tether off somehow, so the police won't locate his body. She grabs the shovel and the bone saw from her venison table, carries them to her rowboat, tosses them in, and rows a hundred fifty feet across the current to the other side. She ties up to a fallen willow near Uncle Cal's hunting shed, where the trouble occurred. This is the first time she's been on the Murray property in almost a year. She climbs the bank, ignoring a sick feeling as she passes the shed, and makes her way across toward the Murray farmhouse. There she sees how Cal's new white Chevy Suburban is sunk down on flattened tires. Cal stands alongside the vehicle, yelling at the banged-up back end of Strong's departing Ford.

"Strong, you son of a bitch! Those were brand new tires!"

Cal's wife stands beside him, wearing a dress with pockets, holding an apple in one raw-looking hand and a peeler in the other. Marylou feels bad she didn't consider Anna when she was thinking about burying Cal. Marylou wonders if Anna is making pies for the party.

Tuesday, two days before Thanksgiving, Strong comes home from work to find Marylou dragging the warm, soft body of an eight-point buck by the antlers across frozen leaves, toward the venison table. She has to stop and rest every few feet.

"Marylou, what the hell are we supposed to do with all this meat? We've got no room in the freezer." He shakes his head. "Even if you aren't going to talk, child, you've got to listen."

Strong would be even madder if he knew she shot the deer across the river, because he doesn't want her to set foot on that bank for any reason. But Marylou was on her side of the river, watching the shed, puzzling through a few things, when the buck came high-stepping down the trail to the river's edge. Marylou aimed the shotgun and calmly fired. She wasn't sure she could hit at that distance, but the buck collapsed to his knees on the sand, then to his chest. She carried the knife across with her, dreading the prospect of finishing him off, but by the time she got there, he was dead. Dragging the buck into the wooden rowboat was difficult, and she was lucky nobody saw her. He was bigger than she realized, and the weight across the prow made it hard to fight the river current.

"Listen," Strong says. "The Murrays could make one phone call, and if those DNR sons of bitches open our freezer, we're in big trouble."

Marylou isn't worried. The Murrays always avoid the law, always figure they can take care of their own problems—apparently they haven't reported Strong for shooting out Cal's tires the other day.

Strong helps her string up the buck and then stands back. "You are one hell of a hunter, though. You always hit what you're shooting at, child of mine."

Marylou squeezes her daddy around his middle, and he puts his arms around her as he hasn't done in a while. Over his shoulder, across the river, she notices Billy, who is her age, dragging out the pig-roasting barrel from the barn. At last year's party, Marylou ran around with Billy and a whole flock of cousins, and some of the boys spit into the men's foamy draft beers while the men were tossing horseshoes. Billy has gotten tall this year, maybe tall enough to staple an invitation way up a tree, but when he or any of the other cousins see Marylou in school, they always turn away.

Aunt Anna appears by the water's edge, wearing insulated boots and a coat almost as long as her dress. She messes with an orange extension cord to light up the waterproof tube lights before she even starts stringing them around the dock. Last year Marylou helped Anna attach hooks for those lights.

Strong pulls away from Marylou's embrace and turns to look at what's caught her attention.

"I know you miss your aunt Anna," he says, shaking his head. "But don't you even think of going to that party."

Before Marylou can look away, Anna drops her string of lights into the river, and Marylou sees the end waggle and sparkle a few yards downstream. Anna is probably laughing as she fishes the lights from the cold current. Anna has always pulled Marylou out of being serious by saying, *Quit brooding and sing with me, Loulou!* or by letting Marylou bake something sweet in her kitchen, a place with all kinds of sweet smells, like vanilla and nutmeg.

"You don't seem to understand what's been done to you by those people," Strong says. "If you would have spoken against Cal at the trial, he would not have been able to plea bargain down to a damned ankle bracelet."

When her father goes inside, Marylou lets herself puzzle again about what they did to her, what Cal did. She still doesn't know why she followed Cal into his shed—Strong had told her a hundred times to stay away from Cal when he was drinking. Even before Uncle Cal shut the door, she knew something was wrong by the anxious way he was breathing, but she never grabbed the door handle to leave the way she thought about doing.

What the men did to each other afterward was more violent than what got done to her, wasn't it? Just after she crawled into a corner to gather herself together, Strong busted into the shed. Marylou heard bones crunch, and two red and white nuggets— Uncle Cal's front teeth—bounced on the plank floor. The men growled like bears. With all the noise and fury, Marylou forgot how Cal had insisted he had to teach her that afternoon how to dress out a deer—he said if she wanted to hunt, nobody was going to do her gutting for her. When they entered the shed, she was surprised to see it was a doe hanging there.

Anna Murray showed up a minute after Strong clobbered Uncle Cal. First she knelt beside Marylou and said, "What's the matter, honey? What happened?" But when Anna saw Cal's bloody mouth, she moved away to help him. Then Cal sputtered those words Marylou has just remembered. "The little slut lured me in here," Cal said. "And don't let her tell you any different." After that, Anna didn't look at Marylou anymore.

Cal had busted open Strong's cheek, and later at the hospital they shaved off his beard for the stitches. Marylou hardly recognized him as her father—going home with him afterward was like going home with a stranger. He hasn't grown his beard back because of his new job, which pays only about half what he made at Murray Metal Fabricators. The nakedness of his face still sometimes startles Marylou.

On Thanksgiving morning, Strong says, "I can't have you killing any more deer, child. I'm taking the shotgun with me. I'll be home from work at six." He slides the twelve-gauge into its case and hangs it in the truck's window rack. His old job with Murray Metal gave him holidays off, and Marylou can't help thinking that everything was better the way it used to be. Used to be when Strong was at work, she could spend time across the river being the girl that Anna and Cal said they always wanted, maybe still wanted. Grandpa Murray used to say that your family was all you had, and that a strong family like the Murrays could protect a person. He said it even when he was sick and dying, said he didn't care what her last name was, she was a Murray.

Instead of stalking another buck, Marylou sits on the bank all morning and watches vehicles pull in at the farm across the river, and she studies each Murray through the scope of her Marlin rifle. After a few hours, Marylou is sick with yearning to be on the other side of the river, to hear the old-fashioned country music from the outdoor speakers, to smell the meat roasting, and to see heaps of Murray cousins wrestling in their winter jackets. She pulls the rifle strap over her shoulder and rows her boat across. She ties up at the willow near Cal's shed. She slowly narrows the distance between herself and the shed as she kicks out rabbit holes in the yellow grass to keep warm. She is listening to the clinks and shouts from the horseshoe pit, wondering what the Murrays would do if she walked over and took a can of pop off the table. But then Strong's truck pulls into the driveway at home, hours before he is supposed to return.

She knows he will see her rowboat tied up, so she runs down the path to the river and waves her arms until Strong sees her, to let him know she is not at the party. As he pulls out of the driveway, Marylou notices her shotgun in the truck's window rack. Luckily Cal is nowhere around. But then, as if conjured up by her thoughts, Cal stumbles out the shed door, looking drunk and sleepy. Marylou silently hoists herself onto the lowest branch of the snake-bark sycamore. Uncle Cal doesn't even glance up as she climbs higher into its leafless branches. She straddles a smooth branch and looks through the window into the shed, looks for another girl like herself who might have gone in there with Cal, but she sees only a skinned carcass hanging.

Cal closes the shed door and steps around to the river side of the building. He puts a red-and-white beer can on the windowsill, and he leans against the unpainted shed wall. Marylou hears Strong's noisy exhaust on the road bridge, but Cal lights a cigarette and doesn't pay any special attention to the sound. Marylou is fifteen feet off the ground, high enough to see her daddy's Ford when it pulls up outside the rail fence a hundred yards away. Cal fumbles with his zipper, and when Marylou realizes he is going to pee right there on the path, she looks away. Then she looks back. Cal doesn't seem to hear the truck door creak open or slam shut. He continues to draw on his cigarette and stare down at his pecker in his hand, waiting for something to come out.

Marylou concentrates with her breathing to slow everything down so she can think better. Strong might kill her uncle, and Marylou knows he would not survive being locked in jail. She also knows he won't shoot a man on the ground, so maybe Marylou should take Cal down herself before Strong gets there, injure Cal rather than kill him. Marylou grips the branch with her legs, pulls the rifle off her shoulder and takes aim at one of Cal's work boots. At this short distance, she could shatter the white radio box tethered to his ankle.

Marylou sights Cal's kneecap. Strong won't kill a man who has fallen forward as though he is praying or begging forgiveness.

She aims at his thigh. For a split second Cal wouldn't know what hit him. A stray horseshoe? A biting snake? Then he would clutch his leg in confused agony. The bullet would continue through the side of the shed, bury itself in a floorboard.

Years ago Marylou's cousins held her down and put a night crawler in her mouth, and Billy once put a dead skunk in her rowboat to set her off. But she always got revenge—she chased Billy down that time and rubbed his face in cow manure until he bawled. Her cousins always enjoyed teasing her, enjoyed her shrieks, and afterward she evened the score, and they all got along again.

Uncle Cal wasn't teasing her, though—he wasn't even listening to her begging him to stop. Over the last year, she has been going back and forth, not knowing for sure if she had begged out loud, but looking at him now, she knows she said, "Please no, Cal," over and over.

"I know you want this, Loulou," he said, as though having him on her was a nice thing, like a hunting trip, like sitting down to a piece of pie. That afternoon, she saw past Cal's shoulder, through the dirty window glass, three little Murray kids peeking in. They looked terrified, and when she looked back at them, they ran off. Whatever they saw scared them enough to go get her daddy from the party.

Marylou looks past the beer can on the windowsill, past the table with the knives and saws, past the newly skinned carcass, to the place on the floor where Cal pushed her down. She has been puzzling about whether he really did push her down, but when she looks at Cal from up high in this tree, things get clearer. A year ago Marylou didn't know about slowing down time to study a situation, to make sure her aim was perfect or to avoid a terrible mistake. Those little kids were two girls and a boy, and Marylou thinks she knows what they saw, what scared them: they saw Cal had opened up Marylou and was gutting her there like a deer on the plank floor.

As Strong reaches the place where the path widens, Marylou realizes he doesn't have the shotgun or even his pistol. Seeing him unarmed now is as shocking as first seeing him without his beard at the hospital. Under his Carhartt jacket he still wears his blue work smock. He hasn't left work for the day, but has just come home to check on her.

Marylou looks through the scope at Cal's eyes, where she sees the same expression of concentration as when he was holding her down, so far from the door handle she could never have reached it. She looks at a patch of Cal's chest—it is amazing Strong was able to hurt such a big man at all. She moves her sights down farther to where a button is missing from his flannel shirt—why hasn't Anna sewn that button back on for him? Marylou moves the tip of her rifle down to Cal's hand, loosely clutching his pecker, from which a poky stream dribbles. She has to do this thing for herself; nobody is going to do it for her. She aims just past his thumb. She knows she is good enough to take off the tip of his pecker without hitting any other part of him.

The shout of her rifle is followed by a silent splash of blood on the shed wall and one last horseshoe clink from the pit. Cal's mouth is open in a scream, but it must be a pitch discernible only by hunting dogs. Marylou grasps the branch above with her free hand to keep herself from falling. The weight of the .22 in the other keeps her from floating up. She closes her eyes to lengthen that perfect and terrible moment and hold off the next, when the air will fill with voices.

Winter Life

Harold had been happily married to Trisha four years, despite Trisha's occasional late night drinking and her bouts of weeping, which had become more frequent since the war in Iraq, where her brother was now on his third tour of duty. Late evening, on the day a blizzard dropped nine inches of snow on their corner of Michigan, Harold was stretched out in bed reading a gardening book. Trisha leaned against the bedroom doorframe to keep her balance and said, "I think I'll call Stuart." Usually Harold would have said, "That sounds like a bad idea, Trish," but this evening he could only shake his head and return to his book. Although Trisha didn't weigh a hundred pounds, he heard the floor creak beneath her all along the hallway and into the kitchen. The wood of these old floors expanded in summer, shrank in winter.

In the kitchen, Trisha made herself another vodka martini. She had dated Harold's best friend Stuart for two years before she'd made the switch over to Harold, whom she'd married abruptly, maybe out of guilt. Although Stuart had a wild temper and although he could be a jerk—he still accused Trisha of being a lesbian because she had several times danced with a girlfriend at a bar—and although he was now married to an on-again-off-again meth addict, Trisha still longed for the intense intimacy she had once shared with Stuart, who was talkative and clever and had been, after all, her first love.

Trisha's heart sparked at the sound of Stuart's brisk *hello*, and she ended up having a nice conversation with him. He asked about her brother in Iraq; he told her that he'd caught his wife smoking meth behind the garden shed the other day. He said that his little sister, Pauline, "that sullen bitch," had dumped her fiancé tonight for no apparent reason. Stuart said the fiancé, Nick, had called him to ask if Pauline was having some kind of mental problems. No more than usual, Stuart had said.

By the time Trisha put down the phone, the details about Stuart's wife and sister were hazy. Trisha didn't like the wife and had never felt at ease with Stuart's little sister, who perpetually frowned. Pauline wore her hair the same way every day of her life—a long black braid—and her hands and feet were as big as a man's. Trisha didn't like the gloomy way Pauline looked at Harold through her thick glasses whenever they ran into her at the Farm N Garden, as though she was always about to ask him a time-consuming favor.

When the phone rang a few minutes later, it was Stuart's wife, who screamed through the wires, "Don't call here anymore, you bitch!" Stuart had said he was deleting Trisha's number from the caller ID, so the wife must have star-sixty-nined her. "Don't you ever call my husband again!"

"Go to hell, crack whore," Trisha said and hung up. She looked out her kitchen window across the unbroken snow cover, lit by their security floodlight. She imagined her brother standing alone in the windswept desert with sand in his socks, and she began to cry.

"Why don't you turn down the thermostat and come to bed," Harold said when Trisha came in and leaned against the bedroom doorframe again, with her lower lip stuck out, arms crossed, shoulders hunched. He folded his book over his chest and patted her side of the bed. "It's never peaceful when you two talk."

"Stuart's not the problem. Stuart was fine. It's his wife that's the problem and his stupid little sister." Trisha tried to stand up straight, but tipped a little and caught herself on the doorframe again. She didn't notice her husband grip his book more tightly. "His wife is smoking meth again."

"And what's the problem with Pauline?" Harold made himself

put his book down. He sat up against the headboard and studied his wife's body. Her smallness surprised him in that moment, the thin bluish wrist, the tiny hand, tiny ring finger wearing the thin gold wedding band, the feet in pink doll slippers. He hadn't mentioned to his wife that he'd run into Pauline today at the Farm N Garden, during the blizzard.

"She dumped her fiancé tonight for no reason, a few hours ago. Listen, Stuart's wife doesn't have to be such a bitch to me," Trisha said, forming a small fist. "She had no right to call up and attack me that way."

"Did he say why Pauline broke up with Nick?" When she didn't respond, Harold patted his wife's side of the bed again.

"Oh, Harold, I can't go to sleep now."

Trisha knew perfectly well Stuart's wife was a meth addict, not a crack whore—it bothered her that she'd gotten that insult wrong in the heat of the moment.

Harold admired that his wife never wore makeup, but he was finding it hard to look at those naked, bloodshot eyes. Before he'd married her he'd been lonesome, but back then he'd focused on growing his vegetables and herbs, and he'd managed to forget for long stretches of time that the whole world was a place of bone-aching loneliness. Looking into her face now reminded him that people were in pain a lot of the time, reminded him he would never leave his wife no matter what, never would create more pain that way. He adjusted his glasses and continued reading about the organic heavy-mulch system. The photos and instructions assured him that spring would come, that he would prepare the soil, that the sun would nourish what he planted.

He felt bad for Trisha this evening, understood that sometimes she needed to talk to Stuart, but he knew the passionate knot of that old affair was too complicated to untangle even in broad daylight, stone cold sober. And after four years, Harold still felt bad about the abrupt shift in his and Trisha's loyalties. Harold and Stuart had always known each other, and Harold had lived with Stuart's family in their farmhouse during several years of high school. Back then, Harold's parents were fighting and fighting with no end in sight. Stuart's mother Mary Beth had not only let him move in, but she let him use part of her big barnyard garden to plant vegetables, his first garden plot.

After finishing her vodka martini in the kitchen, Trisha still didn't want to go to bed, although Harold had switched off his reading light. Instead, she called Stuart's mother, Mary Beth—they had stayed in touch over the years—and at the sound of Mary Beth's calm voice, she began to cry again. "How could Stuart's wife talk to me that way?" Trisha wailed. "She doesn't even know me." Trisha had always taken comfort in Mary Beth's saying that she, Trisha, was her favorite of all the women Stuart had dated.

"Mary Beth, how do I know if I married the right man?" Trisha surprised herself by asking this question aloud. She must have been drunker than she thought. "Is there a right man?"

"Don't ask me, Trisha. I got divorced. I didn't even try to get married again."

"But sometimes I look at Harold and wonder, what was I thinking? All he cares about is gardening. When I was with Stuart, life was more exciting."

"I love Harold like my own kid."

"I know. I'm just having a rough night."

The next morning, at Mary Beth's farm, Mary Beth was talking to her daughter Pauline in the driveway. Mary Beth slipped off her gloves and warmed her hands on the eggs in her coat pockets. She said, "Trisha called me last night, at about midnight. She was all weepy, poor soul. I didn't have the heart to tell her she woke me up."

"Geez, Ma, why is she calling you?" In all the years Pauline had known Trisha, she'd never once seen her on an even keel. Always, Trisha was furious or on the verge of crying or ecstatically happy.

"I've always liked Trisha," Mary Beth said. "She's a loving, car-ing person. Her brother's in Iraq, you know. Talking to her got me remembering one night six or seven years ago when she was staying the night here with your brother. It was February, I think. I woke up to them fighting at four in the morning, screaming at each other, calling each other *bastard* and *bitch* and *lesbian*. Something hit my bedroom door, and I got up and found a snowmobile boot. I didn't even want to be in my own house with that kind of racket, so I got dressed and went to the Halfway House and got some coffee and an omelet. Too bad they closed that truck stop down. It used to be open all night."

"Denny's is open all night," Pauline said, but there was no inter- rupting her mother once she got started telling one of her rambling stories.

"I met a nice fellow there that night," Mary Beth said, "an elec- trician. He'd been out of work all that winter and ended up fixing the trouble I'd been having with my electric ever since your brother Stuart jammed a penny into the fuse box so his space heater wouldn't blow fuses. You remember how that penny melted?"

"I guess I'd better go to work," Pauline said, but she didn't get in her truck, didn't head out to the Farm N Garden, where she would wrestle rolls of barbed wire and bags of corn and laying mash into the backs of trucks for customers. She kicked at some ice ridges in the driveway with her insulated work boot, while her mother went on about dating the electrician, who eventually moved to Florida for a job.

Yesterday afternoon at the Farm N Garden, while the blizzard darkened the sky, Pauline had spotted Harold puzzling over ice- melt products. He was the only customer in the store, although it was an hour before closing. He seemed in no hurry, so she watched him from the end of an aisle, crossed her arms and leaned into the wide, flat shovels hanging there. He read a fold-out label with considerable intensity, adjusted his wire-frame glasses twice, and studied the descriptions of several more products before lugging a box of environmentally friendly pellets off the shelf. He paused to readjust a bottle he'd knocked out of place. When he seemed about to leave the aisle, Pauline stepped up to him. He greeted her warmly, squeezed her hand with his free hand, looked at her as though she were a plant about whose growth he might be genuinely curious.

They had chatted about the snowstorm, about Trisha's brother in Iraq, and about Harold's gardening plans. "I'm looking forward to trying some heavy mulching this year," Harold had said. "And I'll be starting lettuce and spinach in a cold frame." Pauline admired the way Harold was longing for the growing season. She wondered if he similarly longed for the season of fruiting and the season of dying.

She'd asked, "Do you remember when we used to go skating on the pond? Remember how once we skated in a blizzard?"

"I do remember." He nodded, seemed surprised to remember.

Three hours later, after the snow had stopped, Pauline had met her fiancé Nick outside the Tap Room. He seemed, by comparison to Harold, small and foolish with his pink ears—he wouldn't wear a hat because he didn't like the way it flattened his hair. She was surprised Nick even heard her breaking up with him; their voices seemed muffled by the dense white breath hanging between them, or maybe it was the loud music coming from inside. He had gone on in. She had headed back to her little truck with the busted heater, had driven home with her shoulders hunched over the wheel.

Pauline was still standing in the driveway waiting for her mother to finish her story. She took a deep breath and exhaled. She was grateful that out here in the country a person's breath blew away without stagnating. This morning Pauline was wearing her arctic weight Carhartt instead of that flimsy leather jacket she'd worn to the bar. She had not intended to break up with Nick, but she didn't regret it.

When her mother finally finished her story, Pauline said, "I suppose that big mouth Stuart already called you and told you I broke up with Nick last night."

"Stuart called me last night at about ten, asked me if you were having a nervous breakdown or something."

"Is this the most gossipy family on the planet, or what?"

Mary Beth said, "I like Nick."

"You like everybody," Pauline said and kicked at a big chunk of ice that had built up behind her truck's back wheel. "I was thinking, Ma, about when Harold lived here. That was nice of you to let him stay with us while his parents were divorcing. You didn't even have money for fuel oil that year."

"Did I ever tell you about the time Harold's dad threatened to burn my house down?" Mary Beth proceeded to tell a story Pauline had heard twenty times at least. "I told that guy, come on over, at least we'd be warm for a while. I figured I had insurance."

At the Farm N Garden yesterday afternoon, Pauline and Harold had laughed about skating in that blizzard all those years ago—Pauline had been thirteen, so Harold must have been sixteen. Still wearing their skates, they had slowly made their way back from the pond along the trail. The blizzard made it impossible to see more than a few feet, and Harold had taken her gloved hand so they could stay together. Back at the house, they had found themselves alone in the mudroom, taking off their skates, while the storm raged outside. The single-paned windows of the room were etched with frost blossoms, notched ice curves as intricate as Japanese landscapes. Their breath mingled, promised to fill the whole cold room. Harold had been wearing an oil-stained Carhartt coverall that had belonged to Pauline's dad. She'd sat on the quarry tile in her snowsuit, with one foot on the ground, one foot in Harold's gloved hands. The first ice skate had come off easily, but the second one was stuck. Harold removed his gloves, worked his frozen fingers under her snow-sodden laces. She felt the cold tiles under her. Then Harold tugged and the skate came off, and her sock slipped off, too, exposing her bare pink foot to the cold air. He'd squeezed her bare foot and breathed warm air on her toes like a kiss. Or had she imagined that?

"Hey, Ma, does anybody skate on the pond anymore?" Pauline asked, but her mother didn't seem to hear her, just kept talking about Harold's father. She wondered if she'd get her mother's attention if she said, "I love Harold. I have loved him since I was thirteen, and maybe I'll always love him."

At the Farm N Garden yesterday, as the snowstorm blotted out the sun, Pauline had grabbed the collar of Harold's parka and pulled his face to hers. Beneath the fluorescent lights in that aisle full of salt and shovels, she'd stood on tiptoe in her boots and kissed Harold the way she'd wanted to kiss him in that mudroom, the way she'd always wanted to kiss him, even on the day he married Trisha. He had accepted her kiss quietly at first, and she was about to pull away and apologize, but then he wrapped both arms around her, pulled her as close as their thick jackets allowed. He continued to kiss her, stepped her backward and then pressed her against the snow shovels. When three aluminum shovels clattered to the ground, Pauline had to pull away to keep her balance.

Harold blushed pink and swallowed. "I'd better go."

Pauline hugged herself as she watched him proceed through the checkout lane.

Harold felt Pauline's gaze, but he didn't dare look back to see her frowning. He swapped a few weather-wise words with the manager, who stood near the door. He took his wool cap and scarf out of one pocket and his gloves out of the other and dressed for the blizzard. He put up his hood and tightened the strings to cover most of his face.

He drove home at ten miles per hour and then sat in his driveway with the windshield wipers on, looking out over his frozen garden, assuring himself it was still there beneath the snow, fertile and quiescent. Only when Trisha's headlights lit up his rearview mirror did he finally get out of the car.

Bringing Belle Home

A man who trusted himself to own a gun could walk into this place and shoot these guys, one after another, watch the glass fly: Jack Daniels, Jim Beam, Yukon Jack, Johnny Walker Red. The bartender pocketed a dollar-fifty tip and smiled. Thomssen grinned and saluted, but he felt the grin pull tight across his face like a scar, and he might have been saluting the liquor army. He could resist coming here most days of the week, and he rarely came when his son was visiting, but on nights like tonight when he dropped Billy off at his ex-wife's, when he couldn't face his own empty house, he allowed himself a few hours. He was tall enough to see everyone in the place, and he told himself he was glad Belle wasn't there to complicate things.

The barroom chairs, like most chairs, were too small. His size made him powerful, got him instant respect, but he hated that he couldn't walk into a place without being noticed. Tonight he hunkered in his usual corner and tried to look smaller than he was. Billy might end up as big as Thomssen, seeing as his ma was tall, too. That was part of why Thomssen had married Elaine, because she seemed big and strong enough to stand up to him, but after ten years of standing up to him, she'd stood down. She was now married to a probation officer, a man who eyed Thomssen as though assuming he was always on the verge of committing a crime. Thomssen didn't blame his ex-wife, and he had no complaints about the way she was raising Billy—she didn't badmouth Thomssen, as far as he knew. The kid was certainly healthy—he already towered over the other guys on his basketball team. At age fourteen, he was still skinny, though, and nervous and awkward, especially with girls.

The old Dewar's scotch wall clock ran on bar time, twenty minutes fast, but it moved too slowly all the same. Caterpillar hats and John Deere hats dotted the place with yellow and green. Those feed caps wouldn't fit on Thomssen's head, although one year his pipe-fitting shop had ordered a few oversized union local 669 caps for him, and he'd felt so grateful, he had to slip away to the toilet to compose himself. Tonight he wore a wool stocking cap against the cold. Although the place was warm enough, Thomssen didn't feel like taking off his hat or sheepskin-lined vest or his insulated flannel shirt. Keeping his body covered made him feel less noticeable, less a permanent fixture—he might not spend the whole evening in here, anyhow; there was no rule that said he couldn't go home and sit alone in front of the TV, fall asleep at a reasonable hour, be rested for work tomorrow morning.

The door opened and some other men walked in, regular sized, younger than him, kicking snow off their boots in a way that seemed athletic and fun loving. They closed the door behind them, shutting out the cold. When Pete behind the bar noticed Thomssen killing his double shot and beer, he brought out another pair. Thomssen listened to the chatter of guys racking up the pool balls and the sweet crack of the break.

Then Belle walked in the door. Just like that, she walked in. His heart pounded and sent the liquor in his gut traveling, stinging to his size-sixteen feet and his calloused fingertips. A gust of cold air followed her, because she didn't shut the door all the way. She made a racket disproportionate to her tiny frame, stomped her tennis shoes, rubbed her hands together for warmth. After the cold had permeated the whole room, she finally reached back and slammed the door. Everyone's head turned at the slamming, and their looking made Thomssen angry, because he would have liked to have kept her arrival quiet.

Belle walked to the bar and talked with Pete the bartender. The dim bar lights made her bleached hair with its prematurely graying roots look like silver and gold, and with the way she wore it hanging over her face, she could pass for a younger woman. Although it was only ten degrees outside, she was hatless and without a jacket, wearing a big sweater—one of Thomssen's sweaters that had shrunk in the wash—with the arms rolled up into thick cuffs that covered her hands. He would give her his warm vest, he decided, if she'd come over and talk to him. He wondered how she had gotten there. Hitchhiked? Talked a taxi driver into driving her for free? He doubted that her daughter had driven her—her daughter wasn't speaking to her, last Thomssen had heard. The bartender drew her a draft. She looked so small over there at the bar that it seemed to Thomssen he might be able to hold her bird body in one hand.

Thomssen had been the age his son was now, fourteen, when he first met Belle, when Belle's family had moved into the rental house next door. Thomssen's father had been strict and would whip him with a belt once a month or so, but Belle's father was stricter and meaner, dangerous even, and her mother was always sick and stayed in her room. Still, Belle broke every rule as fast as her old man could make them. She ran with older boys, smoked dope in her bedroom, skipped school, and cursed her father to his face. Once every week or two he lost his temper and whaled on her—broke her rib once, knocked a tooth loose another time. Their tar-paper houses were separated by only a narrow driveway, and Thomssen heard the roar of her father's voice, the smack of her father's belt, heard him push Belle into a bookshelf that toppled, heard him kick her into a corner with his work boots. And he would keep on her until she stopped yelling and went quiet. Thomssen fantasized about standing up to her old man, rescuing her, about saying, "If you ever hit her again, I'll kill you." His own dad warned Thomssen to stay out of the neighbors' family business, "Or I'll beat the hell out of you myself," he'd said. "That girl next door is trouble. A grown man can see it a mile away."

"No girl deserves that," Thomssen had mumbled, and that was

as close as he came to defending her. Sometimes after those incidents, Thomssen would wait for Belle's dad to leave for the night shift at the paper company, and he'd slip over and find Belle. Often she'd be smoking on her bed, defiant. She'd offer Thomssen a cigarette, and show him any wounds her father had inflicted. Other times she'd still be lying on the floor like something fallen from its nest. He used to help her onto her bed, put his arms around her, stroke her long, shiny hair, dark back then. He still felt heat go all through him whenever he thought about the way he had failed to protect Belle from her father—his first failure as a man.

The young guy at the bar next to Belle moved his stool closer to her. He looked like Cal Movich's son, Cal Jr., a tin knocker. It only took Belle a minute to slug her first beer, and Cal Jr. bought her a second. She smiled, laughed at something Cal Jr. said. Thomssen could see the baby-faced kid felt lucky to be talking to her. She leaned against the bar, energy surging through her tiny frame, the oversized sweater covering her rear end, her little legs sticking out below it. Those white canvas tennis shoes and no socks. No goddamned socks! She moved her feet a lot, putting one on the bar's foot rail and then switching to the other, probably trying to thaw them out. He wondered if she could have walked there. The thought that she would walk to this bar with no socks on made his heart flood with warmth, because this was *his* bar; there were twenty bars downtown and three or four between here and there, and she had chosen to come here.

They'd spent some nice times here, when they were first together after their twenty-one year separation, a few times with Billy, eating sandwiches for lunch, Belle always drinking more than you'd ever think she could. In photographs, Belle was never beautiful, but in the dim bar light, her eyes sparkled, and her new teeth were white against her suntanned skin. She used to smile with her mouth closed, but the old rotten front teeth had broken off when she'd jumped out of his truck and hit the pavement. They'd been arguing, and he'd reached over and grabbed her bare leg to make her listen. When he'd let go of her to shift gears, she opened the door and bailed, and although he was only going fifteen miles an hour, she hit the pavement jaw first. He jammed on the brakes, but her mouth was full of blood by the time he got to her. In the emergency room, Thomssen had been surprised at how a bruise had appeared on her thigh where he'd been holding her. Each month now he got a bill from her dentist. When Thomssen had seen Belle three weeks ago, she'd shown him how she could bite into an apple with her new teeth.

Although she was halfway through her second beer, Belle still hadn't looked over at him. She knew damn well he was there, knew if she walked over to him, he'd hand her money to get him a shot and a beer, and she could keep the change for herself. The only thing that bothered him was that she wouldn't tip Pete. She didn't have any respect for tradition; she didn't understand how tipping the bartender and being polite and paying child support held lives and communities together. Her dad had beaten all the consideration out of her years ago, killed any pleasure she might have gotten from social niceties. Other people didn't understand why Belle couldn't behave, but they hadn't heard the yelps of pain, hadn't seen the bruises, hadn't felt her shaking in their arms. Sometimes when Thomssen snuck over to comfort her late at night, she undressed him, fumbled with his buttons, tugged down the zipper of his jeans. On those nights she used to lie still beneath him, her eyes glistening, while he made love to her. One day, though, she disappeared, and he never saw her again, not for more than twenty years.

Thomssen had tried to love Elaine, Billy's ma, but he never could muster for her what he had felt for Belle. Rather than fading with time, his feelings for Belle had lingered, like smoke that wouldn't leave a small closed-up room, and he returned to the memories of his first silent and sweet love-making again and again, memories clouded by the haze of his guilt for not protecting her. Then he found her by accident, all those years later, at Gun Lake, sitting on a dock in dark sunglasses, swinging her bare, tanned legs. As she snapped a cigarette butt out into the lake, the feeling in his heart was as much terror as love, as much fear as hope that he could save her after all. They got married, and she called herself Mrs. Thomssen—signed it without hesitation on his checks, on her medical forms. For six months they'd gotten along pretty well. She'd been okay with Billy, if more flirtatious than seemed appropriate. But after that, things had deteriorated.

One moment Belle was laughing with Cal Jr. against the backdrop of the liquor bottles, tossing her hair, and the next moment, she spun around on her stool and looked at Thomssen. He'd been staring at her and couldn't look away quickly enough. She glared at him, long and deliberately, until he felt deformed and grotesque. Her contempt for him was large enough that it contorted his frame.

"Stop looking at me," she yelled over.

"Mrs. Thomssen, you are lovely tonight." Thomssen didn't have to yell; his big voice carried. "Your hair shines like silver and gold."

"Fuck you." She turned toward Cal Jr., who was looking nervously at Thomssen. Cal Jr. was not a tough guy. Belle said, "Ignore him. He's an asshole."

"She's old enough to be your mother, Cal," Thomssen said.

As the bartender slipped behind the curtain leading into the kitchen, Belle swung around again and threw a glass ashtray across the room at Thomssen. Ashes and cigarette butts fell along its trajectory, and Thomssen caught it as it hit his chest, although it knocked a puff of smoke out of his lungs and would undoubtedly leave a bruise. He extinguished his cigarette in the new ashtray and found that he felt inexplicably cheerful afterward.

"You want a drink, honey?" Thomssen called to her across the bar.

"Fuck you, old man," Belle said.

"Pete," Thomssen said, when the bartender returned. "Pete, give old Mrs. Thomssen a drink."

The bartender raised his eyebrows, warning Thomssen, but

Thomssen didn't want to be careful. He pulled out a ten, thought again, and pulled out a twenty and held the bill up between his middle and forefinger. Belle walked over and grabbed it.

"Be sure to tip the bartender, Belle," he said.

"Give me another beer and some poison for that old man over there," she told Pete. She put all the change in her hip pocket beneath the big sweater and carried Thomssen's double shot to him. He grabbed the drink in one hand and her wrist in the other.

"Let go," she said.

"Talk to me, Belle."

The last time he'd seen her, three weeks ago, she'd come into this bar on a Friday evening and gone home with him. Belle had not before then seen the new place he was buying on land contract, and she admired its compactness, its wood floors, and the pretty view of the stream in back. She said how glad she was to be with him. They were going to be a family, he thought after a few beers and shots; together they were going to solve their problems, maybe get joint custody of Billy—Billy was old enough to choose. They stayed together all weekend and finally made love Sunday, in the late afternoon, and then he'd fallen asleep in a blissful state. When he awoke later, he found a note on the table saying she'd gone out to get smokes, and his truck was gone. He'd picked up his wallet off the stereo and found the cash missing, over a hundred dollars. Eventually he'd walked two miles to the Beer Store, looked for his truck, and asked the counter help if they'd seen Belle. With the change from his pocket, he'd bought a forty-ouncer of Budweiser, and he'd walked home with it under his arm. The following morning the cops found his truck run out of gas beside an old factory on the north side. They said he was lucky it hadn't been stripped.

"Let me go, you bastard." Belle tried to bite his arm, but only bit into the fabric of his insulated flannel shirt and the long underwear shirt beneath it.

He enjoyed her attempts at biting him, but when he saw her hand was turning white, he loosened his grip. His calluses prevented him from feeling her skin. Her wrist was smaller and more delicate than the lengths of PVC or galvanized pipe he carried down into holes in the ground or up ladders into ceilings.

"What do you want?" Belle asked through gritted teeth.

His brother, to whom he had spoken on the phone last week, would have told him to say he wanted a divorce. He should have said that he wanted his Visa card for the account on which he'd put a temporary stop, that he wanted her signature on the form to remove her from his checking account, that he wanted back all the money she'd already withdrawn from it.

"I want us to be happy," he said, further loosening his grip.

She relaxed her body and took a long draw from her cigarette. She let it out with a sigh. "People like us aren't happy, Thomssen. I'm a drug addict, and you're a mean fucking drunk."

"Please, Belle, come home with me." He let go of her wrist, and she massaged it with the other hand. He said, "We can try one more time."

"Aren't you tired of trying?" she asked.

"No."

Belle was finally listening to him, and, God, she looked lost. If only she would see she was not lost, but found. He had found her again, the way he always found her after her father's beatings, in those quiet, dark evenings when they lay together in her bedroom, or more recently when he saved her after a drug dealer pushed her out of a car onto his lawn, and he got her to the hospital. She still didn't see how he would always be there for her.

Belle sat looking at him, maybe listening.

"We need each other, Belle," he said. "Come home with me." He was thinking about grabbing her and dragging her out to the truck, holding her arm while he drove one-handed so she wouldn't jump out. He could tie her up in his house, away from the telephone, keep her there until the drugs were out of her system, until the desire for drugs was gone from her blood. She looked scared, not of getting hurt, but scared like she might give in and come home with him if he asked again. Her face looked older up close, and he liked that; when she finally got old, she would have to stop running around. If she were old, the other guys would have no interest, and she would stay with him.

"I'm glad you came here tonight," Thomssen said.

"Actually, I came here to apologize," Belle said. She looked humble, but not defeated. It could be a pose. She might want money. He might give it to her. "I'm sorry about taking your truck a few weeks ago. I'd planned on coming right back, but then I ran into a friend at the Beer Store, and he asked me for a ride downtown, and one thing led to another. I'm sorry."

"It's okay, Belle," Thomssen said. "Whatever you do, I'll forgive you, so long as you come back home to me."

"I might not be redeemable, old man." Her body went limp in her chair. Her apology was intoxicating, but still Thomssen didn't quite trust what she was saying. She might burst out laughing at any moment. She said, "Sometimes I don't know why the hell I go on."

"Oh, Belle." He could not forgive himself for his inaction all those years ago when her father beat her, and he could not forgive himself for pushing her down the stairs in his old apartment this summer (after he'd found out she'd fooled around with his apprentice), but he could forgive Belle, if she was really asking his forgiveness. He leaned in close to her, to smell her, to look into her eyes, although she refused to meet his gaze.

"You'll forgive me for anything I do?" she said. She leaned back in her chair, looked down at her fingers curled on her lap.

"We belong together, Belle."

"We're both assholes," she said. "You think you're not an asshole because you go to work in the morning and pay bills, but you're as bad as me."

"We can change."

"How?"

"With love. If we love each other enough."

"Love," Belle said, with distaste. "If love is the answer, then what the hell was the question?" She laughed in a disembodied way.

"I'm not divorcing you, Belle. I can't divorce you any more than I can divorce Billy."

"If you'll forgive anything," she said, "then you'll forgive what I did last night."

"Goddamn it, Belle." After a pause, he said, "Did you screw somebody?" Thomssen felt his chest expanding, puffing out with smoke he couldn't exhale. He lit a cigarette from the one he was about to crush out and inhaled even more deeply.

"Yeah, I screwed Billy." She looked into his eyes, finally.

Thomssen's body stiffened; his spine extended to its full height. He'd never liked the way she behaved around Billy. She'd sat on the kid's lap one day when the three of them were watching television. He shouldn't have been surprised that Belle had gone with Billy as easily as she'd gone with that apprentice of his. The apprentice had gotten her some dope, and she gave him a hand job in the parking lot of the Beer Store. When he returned to work, the kid had shaken like a leaf all afternoon, and the next day he couldn't do his job until he confessed to Thomssen. Thomssen had forgiven the kid and Belle, too. What the hell was a hand job in this life?

"Billy who?" The liquor churned in Thomssen's gut. He was drunker than he'd thought, had always been drunk. Maybe he hadn't been sober a day, a minute, since getting back together with Belle at Gun Lake.

"Your son, Billy."

"My Billy?"

"But you'll forgive me, right? You said you'd forgive anything." She grinned weakly.

"Forgive you, hell! I should never have let you near him."

His anger was even larger than he was. She stood, but she wasn't quick enough to get away. Thomssen might be big, but he wasn't slow. He worked all day long in the heat or cold, caught pipes before they hit the ground, balanced on ladders, reached above his head to make fine adjustments with a pair of ten-pound pipe wrenches. He grasped her neck in one of his big hands, rested his calloused thumb against her windpipe, and sat her back down. Her chair tipped, slipped out from under her and she was on her knees grasping the table, her pale throat offered up to him. Her face darkened. She did not utter a sound, did not fight him. Cal Jr. and Pete the bartender pulled on his forearms, but they couldn't break his hold. Pete finally hit Thomssen over the head twice with a half-full whiskey bottle. It didn't break, but it hurt like hell, and Thomssen let go at the shock of the second blow.

Belle pulled away and panted until her face cleared and she caught her breath. Then she ran behind the bar and grabbed the big knife Pete used for slicing sandwich onions. Pete sent Cal Jr. out the back door to meet the cops, whom he'd called the moment Thomssen's hand had touched Belle's neck. Belle returned to Thomssen's table and held the knife in front of his face. He grabbed her arm and squeezed until she dropped the knife. The blade fell straight down, punctured the tip of her tennis shoe, and then bounced and sliced a bit of skin off her naked ankle before it settled.

By the time the cops came through the door, Thomssen had let go of Belle, and she was back at the bar.

"He tried to kill me," Belle told them. "Ask anybody in here."

"They damage anything?" the fat cop asked the bartender.

"Nope." Pete righted the chair that they had tipped over. From the officers' casual manner, Thomssen had to assume Pete had told the cops that the fight was between a husband and wife.

"He threw me down the stairs this summer, now he tries to strangle me."

"Is ever-body calmed down now?" asked the skinny cop, licking his teeth.

Thomssen was silent, but he didn't feel calm. He could forgive anything except this. A woman who would do what she did was a monster. The soul had choked its way out of her scrawny body, and now she was nothing more than a stinking, drugged-up whore. His hand had blood on it, he noticed, and over at the bar, Belle was dabbing her bleeding nose with a wet rag. Her wide-open eyes looked vacant. He didn't remember hitting her. Cal Jr. was saying something quietly in her ear. Thomssen considered tossing down his double whiskey, but he thought of the Breathalyzer and reconsidered.

"Isn't it about time to go home, sir?" the fat cop said.

Thomssen realized they might let him go with a warning, no hassle, no Breathalyzer. He could apologize and slip Pete a twenty-dollar tip on the way out, promise to stay away for a while. Thomssen would head home without Belle and let the distance between him and her grow larger. He needed only to keep quiet, say good night, and then file for divorce. He could leave this bar a free man, go home, sober up, and beg Billy's forgiveness for ever letting Belle near him. He'd take Billy on a vacation with the money he'd save from not drinking. Billy wanted to go to Cedar Point amusement park, and Thomssen would take Billy and a neighbor kid he hung around with. All Thomssen had to do now was contain his anger.

But his life with Billy was only one day a week at most, and every other day would be empty, the way his life had been empty after his divorce and before he'd found Belle again. When Billy and Belle weren't there, Thomssen's life outside of work amounted to sitting alone and worrying. His marrying Belle was supposed to have filled his life, and more importantly, it was supposed to have rescued and protected her—if he gave up on her now, he would have failed again. Without him to hunt her down when she was missing too long, without him to take her to the emergency room when somebody dumped her out of a car, Belle would die. If he divorced her, he would not have any right to know where she was. He wouldn't have a right to see her if she were in the hospital. Why wouldn't she let him help her?

Belle shook back her hair, looked into his face, and flipped him her middle finger.

"How could you do that?" Thomssen said, his own voice lower and more threatening than he meant it to sound. "He's just a goddamned kid."

"Whoa, big fellow," the fat cop said.

"At least your son's pretty dick still works," Belle said. "Unlike your sorry, shriveled whiskey-soaked thing."

Thomssen lunged across the room, and the movement was a profound release, an action born of inaction, a way of finally striding across the driveway separating the houses and taking Belle's father's neck in his hands. A way of breaking into that drug dealer's house, kicking him bloody, dragging Belle out of there once and for all, and bringing her home to stay. The cops grabbed him before he reached her, and the big cop twisted one arm artfully behind his back, put Thomssen on one knee with his head bent down. Thomssen heard one pool ball click against another and then no other sounds from the table.

"You see what an animal he is?" Belle said. Blood still dribbled out of her nose, and she smeared it across her face with her hand.

"Jesus, Belle," Thomssen said. He took a deep breath and sighed. "Why won't you let me help you?"

"He wants to help me," Belle said to the cops and snorted. "Ask him why he wants to help me right after he tries to kill me."

"Honestly, Belle. That's all I ever wanted to do, save you." Thomssen turned to the cops. "When she was a girl, her dad used to beat her up."

"Sure. When I was a girl, he'd wait until my dad beat the hell out of me, and then he'd come over and fuck me."

The bar was silent. Thomssen felt his heart stop. That was not what he'd done. Was it? Those tender moments that he treasured above all other moments in his life. The feel of her body trembling beneath him, those glittering eyes open in the dark. Her hands had reached for him; her fingers had pushed those buttons through the buttonholes. Her fingertips had unfastened his jeans. He had not forced himself on her. Had he?

"You ought not hurt a lady, Mister," the skinny cop finally said and cleared his throat.

Thomssen said, "You can hate me. I deserve to be hated. But not Billy."

"I didn't screw Billy, you asshole. I just wanted to see if you really trusted me. If you'd really forgive me for anything, like you said. You won't forgive me. You'll hold everything I've ever done against me the rest of my life."

"Oh, Christ, Belle." He felt his bulk turn to dead weight. What had he been thinking? Billy had been with him all day and all night, and before that, with his ma. Billy wouldn't have gone off with her, anyway. Billy didn't really like Belle.

"Why would you tell me that? Why would you test a person that way?"

"This doesn't seem to be settling down," the fat cop said.

"Why did you really come here?" Thomssen asked.

"Let's get you out to the car. Maybe a night in lock-up will calm you down."

Belle said, "I wanted to ask if I could stay with you."

Thomssen didn't resist when they handcuffed him. He stared down at those bare ankles of hers, blood trickling into her shoe from where the onion knife had sliced her. The ankles were pocked with needle marks; she had used up the veins in her arms, and the rest of her body would fail her soon enough. She would be lucky if she survived the winter without him.

"Go to my house, Belle. You can stay there."

"I don't have a key," she said.

"Let her take the key out of my pocket," Thomssen said.

"There's been enough give and take between you two," the skinny cop said.

"Break the window, Belle," Thomssen said, over his shoulder. "Break the window on the stream side of the living room. Then cover it with plastic to keep the heat in. There's a roll of plastic by the washing machine. The staple gun is in the top drawer in the utility room. And there's duct tape." They led him out into the snow and wind, and pulled the door closed tightly behind them. She probably would be able find his house again, break the window's lower sash, and slip in over the glass shards, unseen by the neighbors. Once inside, she'd turn up the heat, sit and hug herself on the couch, hunker in a nest of whatever blankets were within easy reach, huddle like a creature not quite human, a member of a doomed species who knows safety and warmth are always temporary. She would chain-smoke his cigarettes until the carton was empty, her eyes glassy, furtive, listening for sounds of danger, sounds of his return. She would take what easy comfort she could, but she would not look for the roll of plastic or the staple gun; never in a million years would she fix the plastic over the broken window to keep the snow and cold from rushing in after her.

Falling

On his first day out of the hospital, that no-good son of a bitch Jonas comes walking up the driveway beside the garden. He's got a lot of nerve coming here. Considering he's been on dialysis for a month, he looks okay, although older than his forty-one years. Maybe his neck is a little more bent; maybe his coarse hair has a few more gray strands. Not sure why, but my eyes water at the sight of him. I take the bandana off my hair and wipe my eyes before he reaches me in the bush beans. He drank a cup of antifreeze, the girl at the grocery told me, mixed it with orange juice so he could get it down.

"So you got yourself locked up in the psych ward," I say when he's standing there in front of me. Some women in the neighborhood are scared of Jonas, because he's big and because they see him walking all the time. Some people assume he's mental, but he's not.

He nods, takes a while to speak. "Everybody up there on One North is all cut-up wrists and shit." He's got a bottle in a bag under his arm. He's always been a slow talker, but maybe he's even a little slower now.

Myself, I never could fathom the wrist cutting—so much room for error and for changing your mind, and so much blood. Jonas is sweating as bad as I am, although I've been out in the garden for an hour, trying to save the last beans from the woodchucks, and he's only walked up from the bus stop. I wipe my face and neck with the bandana and tie it back over my hair. I consider slapping Jonas right across his face, but then I might keep on slapping and hitting him, and he might be weak enough that I'd kill him. Or if he took a mind to hit me back, he could probably knock me across this garden.

"You make any friends up there?" I'm wondering if he'll have anywhere new to go, so he won't be coming up here all the time, trying to borrow money or trying to climb into my bed in the camper. I'm twenty years older than he is and getting fat; I've never been anything to look at, but he's been lonely, and there was a time, not long ago, when I wasn't turning him away.

"There was this one big black guy who kept bumming cigarettes from me," Jonas said. "He tried to OD on sleeping pills and some other drugs, but somebody found him like they did me."

Drugs. I have no use for them, not the illegal stuff Jonas and the kids used to cook up in my house without my knowing, not the drugs doctors might prescribe a woman like me, if I was fool enough to present my deteriorating form to one of them.

"You tell that guy where I live?" I ask. I bend down to pick another handful of green beans. My daughter, who lives two thousand miles away, yells at me for bending at the waist; I'm too old to learn a new way to bend, I tell her. Doesn't make a lot of sense to me, the way the hospital tosses all the suicides together in a ward, so they can concur about putting an end to this travail. The beans are freckled with rust spots. I drop them into the paper bag near my feet and wipe my hands on my jeans. Some women throw away beans freckled like these, but they taste fine to me. Last year I processed four-dozen pints in my pressure cooker, back when I had my old kitchen. I say to Jonas, "I don't need anybody doing drugs out here. Not you or some guy trying to OD. I got enough to worry about with Robert."

"I didn't tell the guy nothing." Jonas says it tiredly, as though his not making friends in the psych ward is some new kind of failure piled on top of failing to kill himself and failing to want to live.

When we hear the side door of the garage open, we both look over and see Robert. He hobbles out a few steps onto the brick path leading to the driveway and then rests with both hands on the cane. He won't use the walker. He pulls shallow breaths through pursed lips. Robert's been living in the garage since April. He's got emphysema, he's been crippled since the heart surgery, and he's coming off a long treatment for one of those bad staph infections. It's been two years since Robert applied for Social Security disability, and probably the government assumes he's already dead. Last week he was standing the way he is now with his cane, and then he crumpled, almost hit his head on a brick. Luckily, I was right there and got him back inside and into his chair, and he was okay. If he ever looks over in this direction, Robert will be happy to see Jonas; Jonas might be the closest thing Robert's had to a son, although he'd never say as much.

He'll pay me some rent, Robert keeps saying, as soon as he gets that settlement, but I'm not holding my breath. Robert used to have a cowboy mustache, and he moved so gracefully that when he walked into my kitchen, my legs went weak, but now he's just a broken-up man I'm stuck with. I don't know what he will do in the winter. I don't need anyone with me in my tiny camping trailer, and I really don't need anybody freezing to death on the driveway ice because he slips when he goes outside to piss.

Robert had a room in my farmhouse until this spring, when Jonas and a few of the local kids burned it down cooking their drugs. I was letting a neighbor girl stay upstairs, because her dad kept beating the hell out of her, and so kids were in and out. I told the police I didn't know what happened or who those kids were, and by then the girl had run off to Florida and taken Jonas with her. When he came back a month ago, he was skinny and strung out, his eyes all crazy, and I told him he wasn't welcome on my property. The old farmhouse, the house I had grown up in, the house we had all lived in, had not been insured.

"What's that you're drinking? Soda pop?" I ask when Jonas unwraps his bottle. Used to be Jonas showed up with a forty-ouncer and poured me a cup off the top, and to be honest, I could use a cup of beer right now. He holds out the bottle of grape pop unsteadily, and I shake my head.

"Social worker says I shouldn't drink alcohol." He unscrews the cap with some difficulty, takes a sip, swallows (also with difficulty), and nods. That bend in his neck is probably from nodding agreeably, because he's had to be agreeable to all those doctors and social workers. He nodded at me that way when I told him, before the fire, that there would be no more cooking drugs in my house, so I'm not sure it means very much.

"Why'd you want to do it with antifreeze?" I say. "Couldn't you get a gun?"

"I thought a gun would hurt too much."

"Wouldn't've hurt as much as what you did, wouldn't've cost folks so much money taking care of you."

He nodded.

For myself, I already have a plan. A .22 bullet penetrates the skull, but can't get out, so it spins around inside your head and scrambles your brains like eggs. Maybe Jonas doesn't know about the brain, how all the pain in the whole world gets sent there, but the brain itself doesn't feel anything—hell, doctors do brain surgery while you're awake, squeeze the brain in their hands, cut parts of it away. Maybe there'd be pain when the bullet hit the skin, but after that, it would just be lights flicking out, one after another, making one sad fact after the next disappear forever.

"What was it like?" I ask him quietly. "I mean, before they took you to the hospital."

"I won't do that again," he says. "That stuff was nasty. Sweet and nasty. Every time I think about it, it makes me sick."

"But how did it feel when you were sure you were going to die?" It's something nobody else I know can tell me.

"It just hurt. I was throwing up and then trying to throw up more. My dad said I should call him if I ever think about doing something like that again," Jonas says, backing away from me, into my tomato patch.

He steps on a perfectly formed (although still green) Brandy-wine tomato, and the anger swells up in me again, until I realize I've actually scared him. I've been absentmindedly poking my finger into the place between my temple and the top of my ear, the place where I've rested the tip of my own pistol hundreds of times, pretty much every night these last few months, sitting at my little fold-down Formica table, before putting the gun away and laying out another hand of solitaire, deciding to wait a little longer, just to see what else might happen. My farmhouse kitchen had pine cupboards all around it, full of stewed tomatoes and beans and bread-and-butter pickles. I used to sit with my feet up on the end of my big kitchen table, read *Mother Earth News* and murder mysteries, and drink pots of tea with the sun coming through the window over the sink.

Robert has made it halfway to the driveway, and now he's standing under the branches of the apple tree. *Be careful*, I wish across the distance. I study him for swaying or other signs of impending collapse. The doctors seem amazed he's still alive. When Robert was a boy in the army, he accidentally killed a fellow soldier, a kid from Texas, and spent a few years in jail on a manslaughter charge. He told me the story years ago at my kitchen table, where I'd been feeding him glass after glass of elderberry wine. The sad grace of his confession, with his cheek pressed against my hand, loosened some screw in me that I haven't been able to tighten back up. Some mornings I think there's no reason to get out of bed, but then I see Robert's light come on in the garage.

"You go ahead and call your dad," I tell Jonas. Robert takes another several steps. When I realize I'm holding my breath, I let it out and say, "That's a good idea, Jonas, calling your dad."

Truth is, though, his dad is a useless piece of shit, and a mean drunk besides. I know it, and Jonas knows it. To avoid watching Robert's every agonizing step, I turn to the raspberry bushes, ever-bearing, and pick a few red fruits. Automatically, forgetting how mad I am, I hold them out to Jonas. He takes two, with trembling fingers, and leaves me two. Only one berry makes it to Jonas's mouth. We both study the raspberry that falls like a big drop of blood in the dirt.

"The social worker got me a room downtown. Two guys already come to my door trying to sell me meth." He talks toward my feet. "I told 'em I didn't do that shit anymore. I'm finished with all that."

"For Chrissakes, Jonas. You told me you were finished with drugs before you burned down my house."

"I'm so sorry about your house, man," Jonas says, and he looks me in the eye for the first time since getting here. "If you ever want to build another house," he says, slowly, "remember, I worked for that construction guy. I know how to do framing, and how to put on a shingle roof. I was good at doing roofs."

Whenever I've seen guys putting shingles on a roof, I've thought of laying down cards on a table, and I've felt something soothing in the way they place one shingle after another in a row and then move to the next row, all in straight lines. But the slow way Jonas talks makes me think any house of ours would take an eternity to erect.

"Do you ever think about killing yourself?" Jonas asks so quietly I hardly hear him. "I mean, not with antifreeze."

"Sometimes," I say, after a pause. No reason to lie. But all these nights sitting at my fold-down table, maybe I've just needed to finger the bullets, slide them into the chambers, measure the weight of the loaded pistol in my hand; maybe I've just needed to feel the cool barrel against my head. Maybe that's all.

Jonas nods. He's slept beside me. There's no telling how much he knows.

This was not my plan, but I can't see any way around it. I sigh. "You can stay here if you want, for a while, anyway. Help me take care of Robert. We'll pitch you a tent here somewhere."

Robert finally catches sight of us in the garden, against the backdrop of raspberry spears as tall as we are and some lush pokeweed I've neglected to yank. Robert stands a little straighter when he sees Jonas; maybe he smiles. He lifts a hand off his cane and gestures to us with two bent fingers, but I wish he hadn't. His hips waver, his legs seem unable to support him, his cane slips a little in the dirt. Jonas is watching, too, his trembling jaw setting up, his big body clenching beside mine, until Robert regains his balance. We wave back, as though waving to any old friend, and when Jonas lets his hand fall, I catch it and hold it steady in both of mine.

King Cole's American Salvage

On a windy evening in February, William Slocum Jr., eleven months out of prison, pulled into King Cole's driveway in a Jeep he'd stolen from an apartment complex near his girlfriend's house. He'd cut through the Jeep's canvas top with a utility knife, popped the ignition with a screwdriver, and hot-wired the engine, a trick William Slocum Sr. had taught him not long before passing out drunk on the railroad tracks.

Slocum's car had broken down two days ago, and King Cole, of King Cole's American Salvage, had given him seventy dollars for it, minimum scrap price. That old Mitsubishi Montero hadn't been registered or insured, so if he'd left it broken down on the road, the city of Kalamazoo would have impounded it, but still Slocum felt Cole had ripped him off, had not given him what the car was worth. Slocum and his girlfriend Wanda were now without any car, since hers had been repossessed two months ago. She also hadn't managed to pay her mortgage or get enough methamphetamine to keep herself going since she lost her job, and Slocum hadn't been getting any work either, so things were tight. He'd tried to make love with Wanda last night, but without the meth, it wasn't working, and he knew tonight he needed to hit a lick. If he didn't, Wanda was bound to lose faith in him.

Slocum got out of the Jeep, carrying with him a length of galvanized pipe he'd swiped from Parker's Auto Repair, where he bought meth sometimes and where he'd met Johnny Cole, King Cole's nephew. They'd known each other less than two weeks, but right off, Slocum knew Johnny was a solid guy. Although he was five years younger than Slocum and still pocked with acne, Johnny was generous with the homegrown and seemed like the kind of person you could trust—a rare quality. Slocum had liked the way the kid had asked his advice, had seemed to look up to him.

Slocum knocked hard on King Cole's ornate wood and wrought-iron front door, and in about a minute, King swung open an upstairs casement window and turned on the security light, which lit up the crusted snow. Slocum could see by the tire tracks that the tow truck was the only vehicle that had been there recently. According to Johnny, the man's wife had died years ago, and according to the sticker on the window, Cole had an alarm system.

"What do you want?" King said through the screen. The small man stood with one hand on his potbelly. His long beard and shoulder-length hair were black—Johnny had told him the old man dyed it because he thought it made him *attractive to the ladies*.

"I need a jump start. Or maybe a tow," Slocum said.

"I don't work at night. Call somebody else." Cole started to close the window.

"I'm a friend of Johnny's," Slocum said quickly and backed up so King could see him better. "Your nephew Johnny. You scrapped my old car the other day, the blue Mitsubishi."

Cole opened the window again. "That Jap crap isn't worth a shit."

"That's what you said."

Slocum had stayed up late smoking and drinking beer with Johnny a few nights ago, and when Johnny was stoned, he told Slocum what a cheap bastard King Cole was, how Johnny worked his ass off for his uncle, but the man wouldn't lend Johnny enough money to buy some old diesel truck he wanted. King Cole didn't like banks, Johnny had said, and he carried a shitload of money on him, thousands of dollars in hidden pockets in his jacket. "I should go out to his house late some night and negotiate my own loan," Johnny had said, and they'd both laughed.

"Your car went to the shredder," King said. "What do you want?"

"Johnny's down at the gravel pit. He told me to see if you'd come help him."

"He's got his Nova? Or that damned VW diesel piece of shit he's been driving around this week?"

"Yeah, it's Johnny's Nova needs a jump."

"I suppose if I don't go out and jump him he won't show up for work in the morning," King mumbled. He took a phone out of his pocket. "Kid acts like he's stoned half the time."

Slocum kicked at the ice and rust behind the back wheel of the Jeep, which was idling in the drive. The jump-starting method his daddy had taught him only worked on Jeeps made before 1982, so he'd lucked out finding this old one, and with a half a tank of gas. If King Cole reached Johnny on the phone, Slocum would jump in the Jeep, shift into reverse, and back out of the driveway.

"That numb-nuts forgets to charge his phone," King said. He closed the window and disappeared inside. A few minutes later he came out the front door wearing an insulated leather bomber jacket with "K C's American Salvage" sewn on the back. He wore no hat, so his black hair was blowing around his skull in long dark strands. Looking at him, Slocum realized that King Cole was an old man. Slocum wasn't sure he could do this—he hoped the guy would piss him off and make it easier.

"I think we need a jump," Slocum said. "That'll probably do it."

"Why can't you jump him off what you're driving?" King Cole asked.

"We tried, but it didn't work. Battery's weak. Got alternator trouble. That's why I'm leaving it running now."

"Sounds all right to me." Cole opened the door to his tow truck. Before he stepped up, he leaned out and said, "So you giving up driving Jap cars?"

Slocum moved in. He swung the pipe and hit Cole above the ear, resulting in a dull cracking sound. Cole had a delayed reaction to the news about his skull, and he turned slowly and looked at Slocum. Slocum thought the old man was gathering up some crazy zombie strength to come after him, and he closed his eyes and hit Cole again. The impact made a duller and wetter sound this time, and it knocked Cole down onto the truck's running board. It wasn't anything Slocum had done before, hitting a guy with a pipe, but he kept focused on how he and Wanda needed the money and how the bastard had ripped him off.

"Stay down. Just stay down and give me your money and I won't hit you again." Slocum wiped his hands on his jeans, one at a time, still holding the pipe.

"Where's Johnny?" King Cole whispered, as he pulled himself up to a kneeling position and clung to the truck seat. He got his arm hooked in the removable cloth seat cover.

"Just stay down," Slocum said, but the old man grabbed for the bottom of the steering wheel. Slocum thought about Wanda's green eyes and her milky skin and the way her arms and legs wrapped around him, how she always had something smart and funny to say, and he hit King Cole a third time, a fourth time, and a fifth time. King fell into the snow and lay still. Blood covered his face, soaked into his beard and into the snow around him. Slocum had never killed a man, and he hadn't wanted to kill this man, so he thought about buying carts full of groceries for Wanda's kids and getting them medicine for their ear infections.

Slocum unzipped Cole's jacket, found pockets containing stacks of twenties, fifties, hundreds. He didn't bother with the envelope full of checks. He reached into Cole's pants' pockets, took a wad of bills from each side. The money didn't all fit in the pockets of Slocum's jacket and jeans, so he pulled off a hunk of ones and let them fly in the wind, let them slap against the naked-lady statue and catch in the bare bushes.

He left the man in the snow beside the tow truck and backed down the gravel driveway lined with pines, felt relief when the Jeep's tires hit asphalt. An hour later, he entered Wanda's house by the kitchen door, quietly so as not to wake the kids. She was lying on the couch holding a book on her chest. When she sat up, he tossed the cash and a bag of meth he'd bought onto the velvety cushion beside her. She put the book down.

"There's your house payment, babe."

"Look at you," she said, but she was looking at the money. With two fingers she lifted a fifty-dollar bill from the stack and held it away from herself. "Willie, this money's covered with blood."

"Sorry about that." Slocum looked at his hands, which were also covered with blood.

"We can wash it in the sink," Wanda said.

"How are the kids?"

"They're not here. My sister took them for the night because some bitch from Social Services came by. I want to know who the fuck reported me."

"I can't imagine who would do that, honey."

"Well, somebody did. I told the bitch if she didn't have a warrant she'd better get the hell off my property."

"You don't got to worry about nothing anymore. I'm going to take care of you."

"Yeah, right, Willie. You're a regular knight in shining fucking armor."

When Wanda noticed the plastic bag, she raised her eyebrows, slid out the tinfoil package, and unfolded it.

"Something's shining here," she said cheerfully and patted the couch, inviting Slocum to sit beside her. "Shall we smoke it, my dear? Or shall we shoot it?"

Some people said Wanda was mean, but Slocum loved his woman, loved that he could enter her house without knocking, loved the smart, funny things she said. He would do anything for her.

Johnny Cole stopped answering the salvage yard phone the next morning, because he was tired of trekking into the pole building to say King hadn't shown up yet. It wasn't any warmer inside, because King wasn't there to start the fire in the wood stove. At ten o'clock, Johnny began stripping an Oldsmobile: catalytic converter for its platinum, starter to sell to the rebuild guy, aluminum radiator good enough to resell rather than scrap, tires too worn to bother with. On other cars he might save hood ornaments or yank carburetors if they were Holley or Edelbrock. Even stainless steel brake lines sometimes, when the scrap price was high, although the brake fluid would chew up your flesh. Johnny liked that piles of what looked like junk to most people could be worth real money.

King refused to let Johnny part out foreign cars. Johnny complained about this policy every time somebody came in asking for Honda hubcaps or VW wheels, but King stuck to it. If he towed those cars at all, he took them directly to the shredder, although it meant less money. Johnny didn't see the difference nowadays, American or Japanese or German. The old diesel VW truck he was fixing up had been made in Pennsylvania, according to the door sticker, and Toyota had recently opened a plant in Kentucky. Slocum had said to Johnny that they should go down there and get jobs, except that Wanda couldn't legally take her kids out of state.

At eleven o'clock, King still hadn't shown up and wasn't answering his phone—never had that happened in the years Johnny had worked for him—so Johnny closed and locked the yard's stockade gate and drove out to King's. There, he found the tow truck with its door hanging open, the bushes decorated with dollar bills, and King Cole lying beside the driveway like a bundle of frozen, bloody rags. Johnny fell to his knees in the snow.

After three brain surgeries, the doctors determined that Johnny's uncle was most likely going to live. Johnny's ma, who was King's sister, came and went, said there was no sense in just sitting there, but Johnny stayed in the hospital waiting room, drinking coffee and sharing news of King's condition with everyone who stopped by—mostly women King flirted with and salvage yard regulars.

Johnny had never been part of a medical trauma, and he thought somebody should stay alert so that the doctors and nurses would stay alert, too. Early evening on the fourth day, King's daughter arrived from Virginia, and so Johnny headed to Parker's garage to get himself something stronger than coffee. When he pulled in the driveway, one bay door was open despite the cold, and Slocum was walking out toward a Ford Bronco. Johnny parked and stumbled in his hurry to reach him.

"I'm glad to see you," Johnny said. "I really need to talk to somebody."

"Hi, Johnny." Slocum's eyes were bloodshot. "You look all dragged out, man."

"I've been at the hospital for four days, haven't even taken a shower. Did you hear what happened to my uncle? He got robbed and beat up bad, man, real bad. He's in a coma."

"Yeah, I heard about it. Keep your voice down, Johnny."

"There was so much fucking blood, man, and his face—" Johnny choked, but managed to hold back tears. "His brain was coming out through a hole in his head. They're saying that even if he lives he might be a vegetable for the rest of his life."

"It was bound to happen, Johnny, a guy going around with all that cash. You'd have taken the money yourself if you'd had the balls."

Johnny had hardly eaten in days, and he felt so dizzy suddenly that he had to reach out and support himself on the Bronco. He said, "You didn't do it, Slocum. Did you?"

Because Johnny was small, guys often treated him like a kid, but Johnny had felt a real kinship with Slocum. They'd shared dope and forty-ouncers and stories about missing fathers, about cops and bosses. Johnny had told Slocum how he felt beat down. Slocum had said Johnny had to stick to his principles no matter what. When Johnny had said he didn't know what his principles were, Slocum had laughed, and Johnny had joined in laughing.

"People do what they have to do, Johnny," Slocum said and opened the driver's-side door of the Bronco. "You can understand that."

"Slocum, man, we were just talking that night, you and me, saying crazy shit. I never wanted King to get hurt."

"Listen, Johnny, you told me your uncle was screwing you over. Then the very next day he ripped me off on my car."

"But the cops are saying this was attempted murder. A person could go to jail for life." Johnny didn't feel afraid, despite what Slocum might be capable of doing, despite Slocum's weighing twice as much as he did. Johnny wanted to keep talking until they figured this out, until Johnny could know Slocum was not the monster guilty of this crime. If they talked long enough, they would find the misunderstanding. And King might wake up any minute now and be okay.

"Listen, Johnny, don't you think about turning me in. You turn me in, you're going down, too. If I did it, then you were in on it from the start."

"What are you talking about? I didn't do anything."

"I thought you were solid, Johnny. If I think you turned me in, I won't take it lying down. If I'm taking the stand, you're going to be the pimple-faced son of a bitch I point out to everybody as my accomplice. Don't you doubt it for a minute."

"But I was just talking that night. We were stoned, Slocum, just saying whatever came into our heads."

"I meant everything I said," Slocum said, "and I wouldn't have said it if I didn't think you knew what it meant to be a friend. Listen, Johnny, I've got to get back to Wanda now. Social Services is trying to take her kids away, and she's losing it."

Johnny didn't go into the garage. He watched Slocum peel out of the driveway, and he got into his Nova. On the way back to the hospital, he pulled into a gas station. He could barely see the numbers on the pay phone when he punched 911. He told the operator

Slocum might have beaten up King, and then he hung up. In the hospital parking lot, he imagined Slocum's hands on his neck. He leaned out of the driver's side door and puked.

"It's a miracle Mr. Cole's alive," a doctor testified at Slocum's trial ten months later. He said King Cole survived because he'd been lying on his side in densely packed snow, so that the cold and the pressure had minimized the bleeding. The doctor said that Cole didn't freeze to death because he'd managed to pull the truck's seat cover over his body and he'd held his hands against his belly. The doctor explained to the jury that Cole would never fully regain his lost verbal and cognitive abilities or his sense of smell or taste. On cross-examination, the doctor said he was indeed surprised that King Cole had resumed driving his tow truck.

Johnny was sitting beside King. He took off his VW cap, wished for King's sake he had worn his Chevy Like a Rock hat. He put his cap back on, tried to stop his foot from tapping. King sat motionless beside Johnny, and although the courtroom was plenty warm, he wore a new insulated leather American Salvage jacket like the one he had been wearing when he was beaten up, but Johnny carried the cash now, deposited it in the bank each night. Scars the color of power-steering fluid stood out along King's hairline on the left side, from Slocum's pipe and the surgeons' tools. His hair and beard were coming in gray, and Johnny needed to remind him to go to the barber to get his black touched up—King seemed to feel better when he at least looked the same as before. For King Cole it had been ten months of learning again how to dress himself, how to shop for food, and how to force his mouth and tongue around words that used to come easy.

For Johnny it had been ten months of working by himself in the salvage yard, scrapping out metal, cleaning up and organizing the place. It had been ten months of sick anticipation, waiting for the cops to pick him up, but they never did, and Johnny never heard a word from Slocum, who was no doubt saving everything for the courtroom. Johnny's acne kept getting worse, and he'd weighed only a hundred and twenty pounds last time he stepped onto the scrap scale.

King took the stand on the first day. Under questioning, in his slurred speech, he said, "I guess my brain's messed up. I don't talk right anymore."

"How are you doing with your alphabet?" the prosecutor asked.

"I got *a*, *b*, *c*, but not what comes next," King said, stroking his long beard and then shaking his head in frustration. "I know it, but can't spit it out."

"What about writing? Can you write?"

"My nephew Johnny has to write shit down for me."

When the prosecutor asked King how his life had changed as a result of the beating, King said, "The ladies don't act the same with me. They don't want nothing to do with me except to feel sorry for me."

Johnny knew that several women had offered to help King, even to stay with him when he first came home from the hospital, but he told them he needed no help. Now that King's daughter had gone back to her husband and kids in Virginia and Johnny's ma had moved to Ohio with Johnny's little sister, King would accept help only from Johnny, and then only if Johnny made it seem like no big deal. First thing Johnny did every day, since they had re-opened the salvage yard to regular business three months ago, was call King and tell him to wake up and eat some breakfast. When King got to the yard, Johnny checked that his buttons were buttoned right and his paperwork was in order for the shredder, where he hauled the cars after Johnny stripped them.

The defense lawyer looked like a drinker, Johnny thought, like someone who would come home with his ma from the bar and slip out before morning. He asked King, "What do you remember about the afternoon and night of the assault?"

"I don't remember nothing after lunch," King said. Johnny could see he was making an effort to pronounce each word.

"So you don't remember seeing Mr. Slocum at all that day. Is that right?"

King always claimed to remember nothing, but Johnny wondered if someday a brain cell would reignite, the way a fire you thought was out sometimes left a spark that could rekindle and burn a house to the ground. When Johnny had finally charged up his phone a week after the assault, he'd gotten the message from King, saying, "Johnny, some big dumb friend of yours is outside here saying you need a jump. Why the hell don't you keep your phone charged?" He plugged in his phone every night now, had not missed a single night since King was home from the hospital. He kept saving the message from King, month after month. At first he'd intended to share the message with the police, but cops scared Johnny, and he never could bring himself to tell them about it.

Johnny slipped his hat off when he went up to take the stand and wished he'd combed his hair once more. He had bought new jeans for the occasion, but he still felt as though he were stained with grease and oil.

"King was curled up in the snow," Johnny said under oath and choked on his voice. He felt Slocum's eyes on him, but he was afraid to look back, afraid of what monster he might see there. "He was beat so bad I didn't recognize him. Head swollen big as a basketball, his hair and beard was soaked with blood and his face was mashed." Johnny's heart pounded as he spoke. "I begged him to be alive. I turned him over and there was gray stuff coming out the hole in his head, and I could smell the blood. Then I saw he was breathing." Johnny had thought the blood and brains smelled like metal and chemicals, something from the salvage yard.

Johnny wiped at his face and felt Slocum still staring at him, probably enjoying dragging all this out. As far as Johnny could figure, until a year ago, nothing he had ever done or said had made any difference in this life. But what he'd said to Slocum that night at Parker's about his uncle's money being in his jacket meant everything, and what he said in this courtroom today meant everything else. Johnny testified that King was different since the assault, that he hardly joked, that he got frustrated and sometimes got lost. Johnny said, "King can't say *ten* no more. He says *two fives*. He can't say *radiator*. He says *that thing in the car you put water in*."

The prosecutor asked, "Did you know the defendant, William Slocum Jr.?"

Johnny meant to say yes, he knew Slocum, and then he would say, yes, he'd told Slocum about the money, but that was all. Johnny would explain how he would never have hurt his uncle. He tried to form the word *yes*.

"No," Johnny said. "I mean, I know who he is, but I don't really know him."

Slocum crossed his arms over his chest. In his creased green dress shirt, Slocum was the biggest person in the courtroom, bigger even than the cop sitting next to the prosecutor.

The case against Slocum hit its stride on the second day, when the prosecutor introduced into evidence the galvanized pipe. On the third day, Wanda Jones took the stand. Her cola-colored hair curled neatly onto her neck, her little shoulders pressed out against a soft-looking white sweater, and her make-up was perfect. She had a degree in accounting and had worked at a finance company, she said, before she lost her job and took up with William Slocum Jr.

"Yes, he brought me the money that night. He tossed the bloody money down on my couch. I had to wash the cushion afterward."

Wanda chewed on the inside of her cheeks as she answered the questions. She pointed out Slocum when asked to do so.

"What happened to your children, Ms. Jones?"

"Social Services took them away."

"Why?"

"Because of the meth."

"Do you still use methamphetamine?"

"No, I've stopped. I'm trying to get my kids back." Wanda's hand trembled when she pushed her hair over her ear. She would not look at Slocum. She kept her eyes downcast in a way that Johnny thought made her look pretty, and she hardly opened her mouth when she talked. Slocum stared at her as though she were a life raft out of his reach and drifting farther and farther from him in the water.

Her testimony went long, because the prosecutor had her read aloud from a letter Slocum had sent from jail suggesting that he might try to escape during the trial. "Have your car parked on a main road. Please be ready to help me, Wanda. Please don't betray me," the letter said. "Burn this letter. I love you more than my own life."

"Do you love Mr. Slocum?" the prosecutor asked.

"No. He's a pig."

"Why were you with him?"

"For the meth."

"Did you encourage Mr. Slocum to rob Mr. Cole to make your house payment?"

"No. I told him to get a job."

On cross-examination, Wanda Jones admitted that she hoped testifying would help her get her kids back. When asked again if she had encouraged Slocum to steal money for her, she said, "I never told him to steal it. He got the idea from the junk man's nephew." She pointed at Johnny. "Hatchet face over there."

The prosecutor and the big police officer glanced over at Johnny.

Johnny shook his head no. Wanda crossed her arms, and her lips peeled back to reveal gray-brown teeth to the courtroom. She said, "Oh, you think you're so good and holy, taking care of your uncle. You're just as bad as Slocum."

The judge, a slim, gray-haired man about King Cole's age, said, "Please just respond to the questions, Ms. Jones."

People in the room looked at Johnny. Everybody except King looked at Johnny. King kept staring at Wanda, as though fascinated by her doll-like figure. The judge announced that Slocum, the final witness, would testify after lunch recess. Johnny considered getting into his Nova and driving south to Ohio or Kentucky. Instead he drank a bottle of pop and smoked cigarettes with a courthouse custodian. When it was time, he slogged back into the courtroom and sat beside King.

Slocum felt like a bull for slaughter swaying above his shackled ankles as he shuffled to the witness stand. His dress shirt and khakis were wrinkled. He had demanded a jury trial on principle, had refused a plea bargain, but now the evidence against him was overwhelming. They'd found the pipe with fingerprints and bloody hair where he'd dropped it through the ice on the Kalamazoo River— who could have known there were two layers of river ice with an air space between them?

"How do you feel about Wanda Jones?" his lawyer asked him.

"I loved that woman. I gave her everything, all the money I had," Slocum said. Wanda was no longer in the courtroom, but he tried to conjure her, to get one more look at her. "I never loved a woman the way I loved her. Everything I did was for her or the kids. Them kids aren't mine, but I took care of them like they were mine."

Between his words, Slocum could hear himself moaning like an old woman or an animal, as though something wretched in him, something like regret or sorrow, was trying to get out through his voice.

"Did she ask you to rob Mr. Cole to pay her mortgage?"

"I was her one-man army," Slocum said. He didn't know how much longer he could keep going without breaking down. His ache felt so big inside him that no amount of meth or pot would soothe him ever again. "I was her knight in shining fucking armor. She needed money so she wouldn't lose her house. I had to get it for her."

The judge interrupted. "Please just answer the question, Mr. Slocum."

"No, she didn't ask me to rob him." He should have seen this coming—Wanda hadn't written to or visited him in jail for months—but somehow he hadn't seen it coming. Her betrayal was like punches to the head and the kidneys and the gut, and he couldn't punch back.

"Were you trying to kill Mr. Cole?" his lawyer asked.

"No, man. I wasn't. If he just would've stayed down when I told him to I would have stopped hitting him," Slocum said. He needed to be alone right now. He regretted testifying—his lawyer had advised against it, but he'd insisted. "The old guy just wouldn't stay down." Slocum looked around the courtroom, hoping, but not expecting, to find someone there who would understand. He saw Johnny staring at him. Slocum met Johnny's gaze, asked him wordlessly, begged him with his eyes: "*You* understand, don't you? *You* if nobody else."

Slocum saw Johnny nod, just barely. He saw concern in Johnny's face. It was the first time anyone had looked at Slocum in this courtroom with anything other than scorn. Slocum wanted to shout that he wasn't a hateful person, that he'd loved someone with all his heart, but all he could do was look at Johnny. The acne on the kid's face made Slocum feel sorry for him, for that mean crack Wanda had made, *hatchet face.*

Johnny nodded to Slocum, not in agreement with anything he was saying, but because he realized that the man was indeed a monster and that he was also a regular guy like Johnny, the same guy Johnny had talked to until four in the morning. Slocum was a screwup, the way Johnny was a screwup, only much worse. Slocum should go to prison for life, but that didn't mean he was all that different from Johnny or anybody else.

When Slocum's lawyer asked whether he'd had an accomplice, Slocum finally looked away from Johnny. He did not hesitate before answering. He said, "No."

"Why would Ms. Jones say Johnny Cole was involved?"

He said, "Maybe she wants to hurt the guy for some reason. I don't know."

Johnny squeezed his eyes shut. When he opened them again, he couldn't believe he was still sitting upright on the long wooden pew, and nobody was looking at him.

Johnny noticed that King, sitting beside him, was abnormally fixated on Slocum. King's eyes widened and his left hand began to shake. His right hand clutched the seat beneath him. King must have finally realized in his gut that he was facing his attacker. Johnny slid closer to King. He elbowed him gently and offered him a breath mint. King declined, but Johnny saw it was enough to break the spell. It didn't take much, really, to keep King on an even keel, but the concern he felt for his uncle gave Johnny a tired feeling, like he was growing old fast.

Closing arguments were over before noon—Slocum's lawyer asked the jury to find his client guilty of aggravated assault rather than attempted murder—and Johnny went back to work and started scrapping out a Lincoln Town Car. King was watching him, and it made Johnny conscious of his own breath forming a cloud that hung around him, a cloud that kept him down here on the oily, hard-packed dirt of the salvage yard, down here wearing his greasy clothes, picking through the piles of engines and axles with his filthy hands, down in this neighborhood of ramshackle houses with dogs barking in the torn up yards.

Johnny jacked up the back end of the Lincoln, pried off the passenger-side hubcap and spun off the lug nuts. The wheel did not come right off, so Johnny swung the sledgehammer. The wheel flew six feet and landed in the slush right next to King, splashing him.

"Sorry, man," Johnny said, but he thought he couldn't take King's silence. At least Slocum would have guys to talk to in prison, probably some bored cellmate who'd be awake at four in the morning. Johnny said, "I don't know if I can stay here, King. Every day there's guys coming through that gate who'd kill me for the money in my pockets. And it ain't even my money."

King's phone rang, interrupting Johnny, and Johnny was glad. He hadn't known what was going to come out of his own mouth next. King listened blankly to the first ring, stroked his beard on the second ring, picked the phone out of his pocket on the third, and answered on the fourth. All the while he stared at the sledgehammer in Johnny's hands.

"Okay, half hour," Cole said into the phone. He became alert in matters of towing, often sounding like his old self. "Hold on, let my nephew write down the address."

He held the phone out to Johnny, more hesitantly than usual. Johnny left the sledgehammer standing up by itself and wiped his hands on his jeans. He spoke to the woman on the other end for a while and wrote down directions. He told her, "If King don't show up in an hour, you call the shop."

He handed the phone back to his uncle and said, "King, that woman has a Honda with a blown engine. Why don't you bring it here instead of taking it to the shredder?"

King was forming a response, but Johnny didn't wait as he usually would have.

"Please King, just tow the damned *Jap scrap* back to me. Guys are coming in here all the time asking for parts we don't got. Something's got to change around here."

After a long pause, King said, almost without slurring, "Sure. No big deal."

King did not get right into his truck. He stood watching while Johnny hoisted up the Lincoln's front end and hacked away at the pipe on both ends of the catalytic converter, practically brand new. Johnny twisted it free and tossed it across the yard. Both he and King watched the cylinder arc ten feet in the air and momentarily capture the cold sunlight. It landed with a resounding clang on the pile of catalytic converters—mostly they were dirty and rusted from the slush and mud and road salt, but each of their bodies contained a core of platinum.

Storm Warning

Big Bob stood at the prow of Doug's sixteen-foot MerCruiser with the rebuilt 302 engine and offered up a cold, dripping can. Doug kept his right hand on the wheel and caught the beer left-handed with a wet smack. He glanced behind him to see if his girlfriend, Julie, had witnessed his fine catch, but she was engrossed in her magazine article about the history of salt. On the other side of the back seat, Bob's wife, Sharon, clutched a plastic tumbler and stared dully toward the center of Big Foot Lake.

At slower speeds, Julie, who'd been on the college swim team before dropping out, had been known to slip over the side without warning, so Doug liked to keep an eye on her. While she read, Doug admired her curving legs and her shoulder muscles and the contours of her face, all of which made him think of Lake Michigan dunes. He had read enough *Popular Science* to be aware that the universe might be curved and finite, but he didn't realize until now that the great expanse was probably shaped like a woman.

Doug took a crisp draw from the beer and tried to dismiss such a stupid thought, telling himself the universe was just stars and planets and the empty space between them. He looked through his binoculars toward shore. Cocoa-buttered girls were stretched out on the public beach in apparently random alignments, but maybe if a weather satellite zoomed in on one of those bodies and then zoomed back out, the photos would show the curving beach itself was another woman, a fractal image made up of the particulate sunbathers. All the beaches pressed together might form female landmasses, female continents, female planets and galaxies. No wonder men felt tense.

Doug glanced at Sharon, whose skin was peeling around her bikini line from last weekend's burn. Julie, who was by no means modest, nonetheless always wore a plain tank suit. When Julie looked up from her magazine, Doug was certain she would suggest he stop looking at fifteen-year-old girls on shore and pay attention to operating the boat.

Instead, she smiled at him and squinted against the sun. He'd gone out with her for six months, and until that moment he hadn't loved her. Maybe he'd loved her muscular ass and her long body, and possibly her laugh, which was like waves smacking the beach. But her teeth were crooked, after all, and her feet were big, and her temper was terrible, as bad as his. And sliding over the side of the moving boat was only the most dangerous of her disappearing acts: sometimes she'd get bored at a party and leave without telling him, or else she'd take off her clothes and jump into a strange lake or river. Julie apparently suspected nothing new in the way Doug looked at her; she shook her hair out of her face and went back to reading about salt.

Doug tried to breathe normally, tried to tell himself that he could take Julie or leave her, that it was all the same to him. He lifted his binoculars and struggled to focus on the shining bodies on the beach. He considered that this new discovery of his about the female universe would shake up the study of geometry. Triangles would no longer lie flat on math book pages, but would bulge before terrified schoolboys like the sides of Sharon's turquoise bikini top stretching across breasts too large and soft to be contained by anything in two dimensions.

Big Bob had told Doug more than he wanted to know about sex with Sharon, but Doug had known Bob since childhood, and Bob's generosity and friendship more than made up for his crudeness. Later, Doug would wonder if maybe Bob's big figure at the front of the boat had created a blind spot and that was why Doug did not see a purple Jet Ski approaching, or maybe the boy driving the purple Jet Ski really had come out of nowhere. In any case, Bob yelled, and Doug stood and swerved right, crashing the MerCruiser not into the Jet Ski, but instead into an oil-barrel float covered with artificial grass carpeting, moored for distance swimmers.

Julie, Bob, and Sharon flew forward and to the port side, launched from the boat as if by ejector seats to the relative safety of open water, and the boy on the purple Jet Ski continued on his trajectory unharmed. But from behind the wheel, Doug was propelled through the Plexiglas windshield and over the prow to meet a metal ladder and wooden planking in a bone-splintering moment of twisting motion halted.

He awoke feeling peaceful under the water, didn't mind that he wasn't breathing, that he was sinking to the bottom. Julie somehow found him, swam to him with those smooth, even strokes of hers. She lifted his face to the surface, and he gagged and coughed. When a teenaged lifeguard from the public beach arrived, she and Julie strapped Doug to a Styrofoam stretcher resembling a surfboard. Doug felt weirdly calm as they towed him to shore. Despite the restraints, despite the stares of the oiled women and girls on shore, he felt relaxed, experienced a magnitude of quiet that not even the morphine could later reproduce. In the hospital, Bob told Doug that Sharon had gone into shock in the water and had forgotten how to swim, but that he had gotten Sharon safely to the remnants of the oil-barrel float.

Doug had eight hours of emergency surgery, after which he spent seven days in the hospital with a morphine pump. He would walk again, almost certainly, the doctors said, although they admitted learning to walk would be hell for a grown man. He might begin serious physical therapy in six weeks if all went well, but for now he should lie in bed and make tiny repetitive movements with his toes. In part because of the stitched and scabbed gashes up the front of both his legs, mid-calf to mid-thigh, the doctors decided against plaster casts, so Doug was fitted with braces that snapped on and off, their removal accompanied by the tearing sound of Velcro, and he was told he must keep his legs completely straight, even while he slept. Vicodin would control the pain once he was home.

Julie was waiting at Doug's house the afternoon the nurse and orderlies delivered him, and she directed the hospital workers to place the bed at the corner of the living room to give Doug a view of the kitchen door and the lake, as well as the TV. The younger of the two orderlies kept staring at Julie, who was not wearing a bra under her sleeveless shirt. Doug wanted to smack the kid on the side of the head and tell him to pay attention to what he was doing.

Later that evening, Julie cooked a couple of T-bones on the outdoor gas grill and then took a shower and climbed naked onto the edge of his rented bed. Her bruises had already faded, and she was refusing to wear her whiplash collar. She stretched beside Doug on the bed as though she were the shore of a calm body of water.

"It's supposed to storm tonight," she said.

Because the bed angled into the room, Doug had to turn his head to look over Little Foot Lake, which connected to Big Foot Lake. He felt Julie reach into his cut-off sweat pants and stroke him. He saw himself growing hard, but it may as well have been somebody else.

"See, it still works," she said.

"I can't feel this, Julie. I told you at the hospital, I can't fucking feel it." Her legs seemed impossibly long and smooth beside his braces. Julie had probably shaved them with his razor. She'd done it once before when she slept over, and he hadn't said anything, although it had dulled the blade.

"Don't worry," Julie said. "The doctor says it might take a few more weeks to get the feeling back."

"For Crissakes, Julie. You talked to the doctor about my dick?"

"Just relax and enjoy this."

"I'm not your dildo."

She pulled her hand away.

"I want to be alone," he said, and just then he meant it. For seven days he hadn't been by himself longer than a few minutes. There had been no privacy from doctors, busy nursing assistants, and X-ray technicians, not to mention a series of elderly room-mates who coughed and mumbled. For almost a week, visitors had stared piteously down on him. The universe had become a dull, stupid place with his broken body at the dull, stupid center of it. Julie had come every day after work and stayed past the point when she began to fidget—God, she was like a teenager. Each time she had come to him in the hospital, though, the room had brightened and become almost tolerable.

For a moment, however, here in his own house, he wanted to be alone.

"You want me to leave?" She swung her legs off the bed.

"Good idea," he said.

"You need somebody here."

"I don't need anybody."

"I'm not leaving." She stood and crossed her arms.

Doug picked up the binoculars from the nightstand and looked out at some boys in a paddleboat. They moved toward shore a few houses down and stepped into knee-deep water to drag the pad-dleboat onto a lawn. Doug turned to Julie. "Move my bed."

"Move it where?"

"Push it against the wall."

"Then I can't get around it."

"You don't need to get around it," he said.

"To open and close the window."

"I can open and close it myself. I still have arms."

"Fine." She unlocked the wheels and eased the bed against the wall with her naked hip. She was beautiful naked, more interest-ing to him than girls in magazines, which might explain why she wasn't shy walking around his house that way, despite the possibil-ity of the neighbors seeing in or someone stopping by to visit.

"And bring me my magazines," Doug said.

"What magazines?"

"The ones Bob brought me yesterday. What'd you do with them?"

"Those are disgusting. I should've thrown them away. Let me go buy you a *Playboy*." She locked the wheels and wiggled the bed to assure it was fixed in place. As her muscles flexed, her body suddenly reminded Doug of a man's. Her shoulders were almost as wide as his, her arms muscular. After the crash, she had held him up in the water with those arms until the lifeguard arrived from the public beach.

"They're my magazines," Doug said. "Hand them over."

Julie picked up a plastic bag with handles from a chair near the television. "Don't look at those while I'm here, Doug. Please."

"Then leave."

Julie tossed the bag onto the end of the bed, barely missing his leg, and some of the magazines slid down between his bed and the wall. She looked at him as though she might spit.

"Just fucking leave, Julie. I don't need this."

"Fine." She stepped into her shorts and, after a cursory search for her shirt, put on her jean jacket with nothing under it. The naked strip of breastbone showing through her jacket gave Doug a feeling like a kick in the chest. She apparently wasn't going to button it. He felt his mouth moving, but couldn't speak. He looked away, out onto the lake, at the curved shape of the opposite shoreline. He imagined he could feel the water sloshing around his bed.

Julie knelt and buckled her sandals, one then the other. She slung her purse over her shoulder, grabbed her half bottle of beer from the counter and slammed the door behind her. The room smelled of her perfume, a flower smell and also peppery, like carnations, maybe. He asked himself since when in the hell did he know how carnations smelled? It was that goddamned hospital.

As Julie's car squealed away, Doug realized he was no longer angry. He wasn't sure he'd ever been angry, despite what he'd said to Julie, and he definitely didn't want to be alone. He remained very still, worrying that each exhalation would send her farther from him. His morphine was wearing off, but he had no pump to give himself more. Beside him on the nightstand, Julie had lined up his antibiotics, painkillers, sterile dressings, and lotions with their labels facing him. A registered nurse would be here at eight in the morning to help him establish his routine of care and self-medication. Although Julie had been doing her best, she was a lousy nurse. A better girlfriend would cut him slack, understand that he was irritable from being off the morphine, slightly out of his mind from shock and stiffness, and fearful at the possibility of being permanently crippled. The intern had told him that there was danger of bone infection—and thus amputation—until every fracture healed completely. In other words, for a year at least. Another girlfriend would have swallowed her pride and sulked in the other room. No wonder Julie had been kicked off her college swim team—she had probably walked out in the middle of a meet, probably after telling the coach to screw himself. And no wonder this was the longest Julie had ever dated anyone. Of course it was almost the longest for Doug, too. With that realization, he felt a rush of warmth toward her, and he drank the entire glass of water she'd placed beside him. Just under the bed, where he could reach them, were plastic hospital bottles to piss into, but he dreaded having to use the bedpan. Julie shouldn't have to deal with that.

The phone rang half an hour later. "How are you?" Julie asked. At the sound of her relaxed voice, Doug felt himself treading water, imagined himself grasping at her, trying to climb onto her as though she were dry land.

"Fine," he said. "Where are my binoculars?"

"I put them beside the bed."

Doug looked at his left hand. He was clutching the binoculars, had been since she left.

"You shouldn't be alone," she said.

"Bob and Sharon are on their way over," Doug said. "They're going to stay the night. Maybe we'll have a ménage à trois."

Julie laughed, and he heard waves slapping the shore. Doug didn't want her to return out of pity or a sense of obligation. When she came back, he'd say Bob and Sharon had just left.

"Where are you?"

"The Pub."

He recalled her jacket with no shirt under it, her beautiful collarbone, her navel. "Who's hitting on you?"

"Nobody's hitting on me. I'm talking to Martin the bartender."

"Figures Marty's hitting on you. So are you going to screw him?" Even as Doug said it, he wasn't sure whether he was saying it aloud or whether it was merely an ugly thought flitting through his brain.

"Fuck you, Doug," Julie said.

Doug considered apologizing—that's what Julie was waiting for. He could blame the way he was acting on the painkillers, but his body became suddenly sweaty and shivery and he slammed the phone down. Instantly he longed for Julie. He couldn't remember if he'd asked her to come back. In any case, she had to know he wanted her there.

The next call was Bob asking if he needed company. "No, Julie's here with me. She's rubbing my dick right now." Doug moved his foot, and the last of Bob's magazines fell between the wall and the bed. "Give me a call tomorrow, Bob."

Doug must have dozed off, because when he woke to pain racing up and down his legs, the room was darkening. Wind blew over his bed, and rain poured onto the windowsill beside him. He leaned up as far as he could and managed to pull down the open window, wishing Julie were there to see he wasn't a complete invalid. The action exhausted him. His surgeon had said there could be blood clots from the accident. Exertion could loosen one into his bloodstream, send it to his brain, and he would pass out and never wake up. He should call Bob back and ask him to come over, but he still held out hope for Julie. He could call the Pub, but he'd never before called a bar and asked for a woman. He whispered to himself, "Julie, I'm sorry," but it sounded pathetic.

When the clock said 9:07, he swallowed a Vicodin with saliva. A window across the room was still open about six inches, and a stream of cool air blew toward him. Trees thrashed above the house. Doug heard a crunch and watched a limb break loose from the trunk of his big burr oak and fall to the ground, flattening a burning bush. For years that branch had hung twenty feet above his lawn, but now it lay there like a dead body between him and the lake. If Julie came back, he would tell her he was sorry, however it might sound.

The surface of Little Foot was chopped with tiny whitecaps, the wildest effect such a small lake could manage. As soon as he was allowed to get wet, he'd have Bob take him across Little Foot and back onto Big Foot, even if it was in the outboard with Doug strapped to a piece of plywood. Things were always easy between him and Bob. Doug couldn't remember uttering a single apology to Bob in the twenty years they'd known each other. Bob just knew when he was sorry.

Within twenty minutes of taking his Vicodin, by 9:27, the drug had taken the edge off the pain, but it couldn't mute the stiffness of his legs. The drug made him sweat, too—he'd only been lying there in his living room six hours, but already he wished he could change the sheets.

He clicked the TV remote control until he reached the cool blue of the weather channel, where a man with the authority of a doctor announced eighty-mile-per-hour winds to the west. The surgeon had told Doug a few days ago that some of the bones didn't heal until you walked on them. Doug had assumed the opposite, that you didn't walk on them until they healed. That's why people didn't heal in the past, the surgeon said. He spoke as though doctors understood everything about healing now.

The meteorologist announced the approach of a powerful storm and said that twelve thousand people in southern Michigan and northern Indiana were already without power. Hardly "without power," Doug thought. Even in the dark those folks could get out of bed and go to their refrigerators for some beer to choke down their pain pills. The Vicodin bottle beside him warned, "Alcohol will intensify the effect of this medication." Excellent idea. At the very least, he needed another glass of water, but there was no way he could get himself into his wheelchair without help. Although he would be willing to apologize to Julie when she came back, he couldn't bring himself to call the bar yet. For six months, he'd struggled to keep even with her, to keep her from realizing she was too good for him. Now that she'd saved his life, the scales were tipped hopelessly in her favor. He stared out the window at the oak branch. How long would that big limb lie in his yard? How long before Julie left him for good?

It was going to be difficult showing his appreciation throughout what the doctors said would be a long ordeal. Thanking people was easy in situations where it meant nothing—when the grocery clerk gave him change, for instance—but desperately needing help complicated everything. He would constantly be thanking people for getting him into his wheelchair and back into his bed, for changing his sheets, for preparing food, for emptying the bed pan, for cutting up that big branch and hauling it away. He stared at the surface of the lake until it became a massive dark organism whose watery shape could be outlined by connecting the dots of light fixed at the bases of docks. Julie needed to try and understand what he was going through. Why was she being so damned difficult?

When the radar-weather voice announced the sighting of a tornado in Kalamazoo County, each light at the water's edge, his own included, seemed like a personal call for help. The calls were all the more desperate for having glowed steadily and unnoticed during the four years he'd lived on the lake. Other than the neighbors next door, he didn't really know any of these people. Everyone on this lake may well be trapped in his own house tonight, Doug thought, at the mercy of the forces of the universe: weather and women and pain. He reached for the phone to call Julie. First he'd try her at home, and then he'd try the Pub. But when he put the phone to his ear, the line was dead.

He looked across the water through his binoculars, into a living room window, and focused on a gray-haired woman with glasses sewing. She did not seem alarmed. He moved laterally to the window of the next house, where a shriveled man with no hair reclined in a bed with white sheets. The old man looked toward the lake or perhaps toward the weather channel on a television placed beneath the window. Or maybe he stared at nothing. Or maybe with every worn thread of his pajama shirt and every cell of his old, withered body, the man was trying to call out for help.

Doug didn't usually mind storms, but that big limb lying between him and his dock changed everything. He panned the shoreline with his binoculars and saw geese as dim as ghosts standing on somebody's lawn, three big ones and a bunch of what looked like half-grown goslings. He wondered where other animals went at times like this. Woodchucks must hide underground until their dens flooded. Songbirds were probably already hunkered down on their nests, the mamas spreading their wings out over their babies. The smallest tornado would pick up those geese and spray their feathers across the sky. Get to safety, he wanted to shout, a storm is coming! Doug didn't remember whether he was supposed to open or close his windows for a tornado—he hadn't paid attention during the tornado drills in school. Would glass soon be flying toward him at eighty miles per hour? Where was Julie now? Was she someplace safe?

As the porch light next door sputtered out, so did Doug's television. The leftover blue glow of the screen lit the room for another second and then faded. The lights across the way were still on, but Doug couldn't bear to look at the old man again. The screaming of the wind and the rattling of branches grew in intensity. No way could Doug get himself into the basement for protection—even lowering himself to the floor could loosen blood clots and bone slivers, loosen the screws holding his legs together. As his eyes adjusted to the darkness, he began to make out his own body, his muscled arms leading to big hands. He lifted himself onto his elbows, tore loose the Velcro, and unwrapped the scabbed and stitched legs that had already begun to shrivel and grow pale. He knew he wasn't supposed to take off the braces, but these were his own legs, goddamn it. Doug heard wood groan above his house. Perhaps the big tree stretching up beside the living room would crash through the roof.

"Julie, I'm sorry!" he shouted, in what sounded to him like a little boy's voice. He didn't dare yell again, for fear of shaking loose the branches above him, for fear of further upsetting the universe.

He looked down to where the magazines had fallen, between the wall and the bed. Although it was too dark to read, he wanted to hold the pages and try to make out the shape of a woman. He grabbed the rod that opened and closed the blinds and tugged on it, but it wouldn't disconnect. He remembered the way he had lain so passively in the water in Julie's arms, and he yanked the rod with so much force that the plastic blinds clattered to the bed and then to the floor, taking a long time to settle. He clutched the rod and lay immobile, waiting for his heart to slow, waiting for any stray clots to travel to his brain and kill him. Hail began to rattle on the roof and deck, and crash against the screen of the open window across the room. Doug stretched, but managed only to push the magazines farther away. He felt the rod drag on something soft. He stretched again and retrieved Julie's lost sleeveless shirt. He held it to his face and breathed through it. The lights died in the houses of the old man and the sewing woman across the way. Lights around the edge of the water went off one after another, like a dress unzipping at the speed of electricity along the curve of the lake. Doug's breath warmed the fabric of Julie's shirt, which smelled not only of carnations, but also of honey and sweat and maybe something like milk.

The universe seemed darker than he'd realized, and larger, which made each thing in it, including him, smaller. Years ago, smart-aleck schoolboys like him and Bob should have learned more than their grammar and arithmetic. Why hadn't they learned the way bodies could break and how slow and difficult it was to heal? Heat lightning flashed everywhere at once, and Doug decided he would invent a hundred apologies and thank-yous and recite them until the words flowed as easily as the names of states and the multiplication tables. In a few days, his friend Bob would lug a chainsaw from the bed of his Dodge Ram and walk on legs as thick and sturdy as tree trunks down into Doug's backyard, and Doug would sit in his wheelchair with his legs straight out in front of him and watch Bob cut that branch. Doug could only hope he wouldn't weep out of gratitude.

As the sound of groaning wood above the house grew louder, hail fell larger and harder, and the air pressure thinned. Doug breathed deeply through Julie's shirt and watched over the lake for a tornado with a slender waist and broad shoulders. The kitchen door blew open. Then it closed against the wind. Even without electric lights, he could see that Julie's hair was wet.

Fuel for the Millennium

The banks were doomed. Hal Little knew it beyond the shadow of a doubt. And without the banks, everything else would fail—the stock markets, of course, but also the government and then the power company, the water and sewer, law and order, and most importantly, the gas stations. People said that stored gasoline soured after a few months, but sour gas was better than none, and Hal already had a half dozen fifty-five-gallon blue-plastic drums of gas stored behind his pole barn.

A few months ago, in the heat of summer, Hal had loaded the first of the blue barrels onto his homemade trailer and had pulled into the Total station, but before he'd pumped even a gallon, the attendant had run out of the building yelling that the barrel was not "an approved container." Ever since then, Hal had been filling the gas tank of his Country Squire and siphoning the gas into the barrels, which he concealed under an old army canvas, upon which autumn leaves were now falling. He was starting to wonder, though, if he should dig a pit and bury any further barrels so nobody else could stumble across them. One barrel had begun to bulge, so Hal had clamped a metal strap around it, and he planned to take fuel out of that one first. No amount of gasoline would be enough, of course, but he figured that if he didn't drive much—and after the collapse, he wouldn't be going around fixing people's washing machines—he'd need only a few gallons per day to power his generator.

Hal Little liked the tall, smiling man whose washing machine belt he'd just replaced, and that was why he decided to make a suggestion. "You ought to get yourself some gasoline stored away now," Hal said as he stood in the man's yard. "It's going to be impossible to get gasoline after the new year."

"We're not worried about the Y2K thing," the man replied.

Hal figured the man was about half his age, which might explain why he was naive about the situation—young people went along thinking that nothing bad could happen, thinking that their parents couldn't be killed in a car crash so bloody that blood would stain the asphalt at that intersection for months. They didn't think Satan could move among ordinary people in the form of a building inspector or a frisky squirrel. It never occurred to young people that the world could descend into darkness and chaos, leaving every man to fend for himself.

"Well, you should prepare just in case," Hal said. "I've got some gas put away, and I'm ordering live chickens from the Farm N Garden so I'll have eggs." Actually, Hal Little was not looking forward to raising chickens in his new pole barn. He didn't like the idea of having to feed and water critters every day, not to mention figuring out what to do if they got sick. But, as he was trying to make this tall, smiling man realize, a person had to prepare. The millennium problem was like religion. Hal's father the minister used to say that even though you couldn't force anyone to believe in Our Lord, you were duty bound to suggest a fellow ought to love Jesus, just in case he had overlooked the importance of everything the Bible said. Hal hoped further that accepting both Jesus and the millennium problem would help Americans recognize the way that banks and Jews and the government were plotting together to deny the impending Y2K disaster.

"We think it's a lot of fuss about nothing," said the tall, smiling man.

"Do you trust in Jesus?" Hal asked. "Jesus helps those who help themselves."

"We're not religious."

Hal stood there in the man's yard listening to a bird singing. Hal suffered from the same degenerative eye disease that had afflicted his father, and it had progressed in the last several years so that Hal had to wear telescopic glasses for driving. Without those glasses he saw birds as only shadowy, fluttering movement. It occurred to Hal that birds must really like people, because you didn't hear birds out in the country near as much as you heard them in town. Here in Comstock Township, before he'd sold the house he'd inherited from his parents, may they rest in peace, Hal had heard chirping and singing from morning till night, all year round. His old next door neighbor, Em Garrity, had gone outside every day in pink slippers and a quilted bathrobe to put sunflower seed in a feeder shaped like a hay barn with a silo. She'd expressed shock that Hal wanted to sell the house where he'd lived his whole life, and he'd explained that he didn't like selling, but that he had to prepare for Y2K, as *she* ought to be doing, too. Em said, "You're a fool, Hal" and dismissed him with a wave. At Hal's new ten-acre property twenty-two miles outside of town, there were no neighbors, and Hal rarely heard any birds.

The tall, smiling man's wife came out of the house with their baby strapped onto her back, and she walked past Hal, close enough that, even without his glasses, he could make out the expression on the baby's face. The baby looked at Hal and laughed and put his fingers into his mouth before disappearing into blurriness. Hal felt bad that the parents were not taking precautions, if only for the sake of that child.

"You ought to withdraw your money from the bank," Hal said. "Did you know that the bank's only got a dollar seventeen cents for every hundred dollars on deposit?"

"I didn't know that," said the man. The sun was shining through a big tree's branches, lighting up orange and yellow leaves, indistinct, but bright as heaven.

"Most people don't know." Hal scratched his head, which was nearly as bald as the baby's. "Everything else—that ninety-eight plus dollars—is loaned out." Hal didn't want to scare the man too much, but he knew that if a couple of rich guys went to the bank a few blocks away from here, Hal's old bank, and asked the teller for all their money in cash, then the vault would be cleaned out, the bank would have to close its doors, and that would make angry people line up outside and start breaking windows. After a while the mob would start overturning cars. Hal didn't have anything left in the bank—he'd spent most of his money on the ten acres north of town, on the pole barn he now used for a house, on the gasoline generator and the windmill he'd ordered, but hadn't yet received. Probably the banks would fail before the new year, because people would wise up and withdraw their money at the end of November, and the government would struggle for two or three weeks before collapsing. Hal had heard on the Faith Channel that the government was printing all kinds of money—increasing the money supply by fifty percent—but that wasn't going to be enough. The banks were doomed.

"Did you know we get ninety percent of our gasoline from foreign countries?" Hal asked.

"No. I didn't know that, either." The man was still smiling, apparently *still* not realizing the gravity of the situation despite Hal's telling him clearly.

"The seaports are the least prepared of all. That's why there won't be any gasoline." Hal held back the worst, didn't say that boats full of foreign oil would be floating aimlessly, their captains not knowing where to go with their controls all haywire. American nuclear submarines might launch missiles by accident and blow the ships up, or the Russians might launch missiles and pretend they did it by accident. Russians and Chinese would likely invade the United States, as they'd wanted to do all these years. Russians and Chinese were accustomed to chaos, and with the government collapsed, they could finally dominate America. They'd try to make everybody renounce Jesus, but they wouldn't succeed with Hal Little. No, Hal knew that hell fires were worse than any pain on this earth, and his belief in Jesus was his ultimate survival tool.

In addition to Jesus and the generator and gasoline, Hal had a chainsaw, sharp knives, a spare set of prescription telescopic glasses, a solar-powered hot-water tank, and sixteen books on survival, including an out-of-print pamphlet from the US Army detailing which bugs were edible. He had not yet bought his fifty-pound bags of rice and beans, because he was waiting until the last minute for optimum freshness. He didn't want to eat rice and beans, but there probably wouldn't be any other food after hunger-crazed mobs broke the plate-glass windows and emptied the shelves of the Meijer's Thrifty Acres and the Harding's Friendly Market.

"Well, I hope you change your mind before the new year," Hal said, "for the sake of that baby."

"How much do I owe you?" asked the man.

"Thirty dollars." Hal accepted the two bills. "Do you want a receipt?"

"Naw." The man reached out to shake hands. "And thanks for coming out right away. You really saved us."

"You're welcome," Hal said. As Hal walked toward his car, he passed the figure of the woman kneeling by the driveway—weeding flowerbeds, it looked like, which would explain the sweet smell of their yard. The baby was still on her back, reaching out his arms to Hal.

Although he'd never gardened, Hal would take this thirty dollars to the Farm N Garden tomorrow and buy non-hybrid seed corn to plant next spring to grow more feed for the chickens. He'd have to eat some of the roosters if he ended up with more than a few, the people at the Farm N Garden had told him, or the hens wouldn't lay eggs. Hal had never killed anything before, as far as he knew, and he wasn't looking forward to it. He'd been meaning to buy a gun, a shotgun, probably, and a couple thousand rounds of ammunition. Although he'd never fired anything more powerful than a pellet gun, way back when he was a boy, he thought he might be able to shoot at unruly people if they came out to his place and threatened to steal his gasoline or generator or chickens.

He knew it was un-Christian to think about killing folks. It was better not to plan on it, but rather to act in self-defense in the heat of the moment.

Hal got into his car, put on his telescopic glasses, and fastened his safety belt. Saving yourself was your duty. If this couple with the baby didn't even believe in Jesus yet, they were probably doomed. Unless they started right away, there wouldn't be enough time for them both to start believing and to make preparations for the end. A Faith Channel minister had prepared viewers for Armageddon two years ago, but that had been based on mistaken information given him by the Catholics, he said, and the minister himself had reinterpreted Nostradamus's predictions to mean that the end was rescheduled for the coming year.

Most righteous people were saying that if Y2K didn't destroy America, doomsday would arrive the following September, but Hal had heard a late-night minister explain how "sept" meant "seven," so maybe doomsday would come in the seventh month, July. At that time, the minister predicted, a meteor a quarter mile across would plunge into the North Atlantic, causing a tidal wave that would swamp many nations, including England, and go underneath the North Pole—probably crack up the North Pole or push it partway around the world—and worst of all, the force would bust open all the oil refineries around the North Sea and send flaming gas out onto the water, so that all the way to America the ocean would be on fire. One by one the oil tankers would explode, and nuclear submarines would spit missiles at populated landmasses.

Of course Hal Little would be okay in that extreme situation, because Jesus would carry all believers to safety. Or if a mob of people who'd already broken the plate-glass windows and cleared out the shelves of Meijer's and Harding's showed up at his property with their torches and pistols, Hal would not leave his pole barn. He had faith that when the situation looked hopeless, Jesus would lift him and his barn right up into the sky, float it like a sheet-metal balloon into the clouds and up farther to the Kingdom of God, where He would set it down again gently, so it nestled into the Heavenly Woods—not right next to the other houses, but not far away, either, from the other Men of God who had prepared for the end. Hal would be pleasantly surprised if he were set down near a Faith Channel minister, or near his own father and mother, both of whom had died in a terrible traffic accident twelve years ago, due to his father's failing vision. It was even possible that Hal would end up somewhere near the tall, smiling man and his wife.

With his glasses on, he could see the man was now holding the baby in one arm, and when Hal looked, the man waved, and he waved the baby's hand. Hal could swear the baby reached toward him again, made a little jumping motion.

Up in Heaven, when Hal opened his reinforced steel-and-aluminum, solid-core front door into the New Holy Universe, he knew he'd hear the sweet voices of birds and angels. He hoped he would smell flowers. He hoped there would be babies.

Boar Taint

The boar hog was advertised on a card at the grocery store for only twenty-five dollars, but the Jentzen farm was going to be a long, slow drive, farther down LaSalle Road than Jill had traveled, past where the blacktop gives way to gravel and farther past, where it twists and turns and becomes a rutted two track. Ernie was finishing the milking when Jill hooked up the stock trailer. He had given her directions already, but before she pulled away, he came out and stood beside the truck and studied her, the way he'd done when she went to Ann Arbor last time—they'd been married almost a year, but maybe he hadn't been sure she was coming back.

"Are you sure your foot's okay?" Ernie asked. A cow had stepped on it when a stray dog ran through the barn that morning, and she was wearing the laces on her work boot loose.

"It's fine. I'll see you in a couple hours," Jill said.

"You sure cursed up a storm." Maybe he was stalling because he didn't want to go back inside the hot barn—it was muggy and smelled of bleach from yesterday's scrubbing.

Jill said, "Let's have tomato and bacon sandwiches for supper."

"You think you got enough daylight? Sure you don't want to wait until tomorrow?"

"Somebody else'll get there first thing in the morning." Jill had seen the advertisement for the hog only an hour and a half ago; maybe nobody else had seen it yet.

"That road's going to be muddy and washed out from all this rain," Ernie said and ran a big hand through his black hair. He was ten years older than Jill, and if he was like his father, he would go gray by fifty and be no less handsome for it. Like his father, a widower, Ernie'd had his choice of women after his divorce. He said, "You wouldn't want to try to navigate that road after December with anything but a snowmobile." He wiped the sweat from his neck with a navy bandana. There was a bright new blood blister under his ring fingernail.

"No chance of snow today," she said and Ernie nodded. Whether it was a joke or serious bad news, Ernie nodded the same way.

"You know, I went to school with a Jentzen kid," Ernie said. "Had only one pair of overhauls to his name. He never brought anything to eat for lunch, not even lard-and-salt sandwiches like us regular poor kids. He still couldn't read in the fifth grade." Ernie folded the handkerchief, slid it into his back pocket. His slow movements worked on her like a liquor, calmed her agitation, even when she didn't want to be calmed.

They heard a long, low moo followed by squeals from the gilts.

"Twenty-five bucks. That's an awful cheap price for any kind of hog," Ernie said. "You got to ask yourself."

Jill nodded. She had asked herself and ignored the answer.

She drove out slowly, so she could keep looking back at her husband making his way into the barn. The man had an easy way of walking that made her think he could walk all day and all night, too. Whatever poor condition this hog was in, Jill would bring him home, quarantine him for a few weeks, worm him, and dope him with broad-spectrum antibiotics. Jill was sure Ernie felt skeptical about this whole plan she had concocted with the neighbor for raising pigs for pig roasts; the longer he didn't express his skepticism, however, the more desperate she felt about succeeding, especially after her last two farm schemes had gone so badly. Ernie kept himself focused on his hundreds of acres of the same corn, oats, and beans he'd been harvesting for the last three decades, and Jill had begun to think maybe she ought to do the same.

She meant to arrive at the Jentzen place in the daylight, but she stopped in town to get some rye bread and, as an indulgence, an imported dark chocolate bar with hazelnuts, something she rarely bought for herself, and then she got a little lost on the unmarked dirt roads. As she bumped along, too slowly to deter the deer flies, the truck steered itself by staying in the washed-out ruts. When the glove box popped open, she leaned over and extracted a pocket flashlight before slamming it shut. The chocolate bar on the seat thrilled her, perhaps more than was reasonable. She would keep it in her underwear drawer, she decided, and eat one square a day.

The road dead-ended into mud puddles in the yard of a two-story wooden house, and one look told Jill that the Jentzens were not hooked up to the power grid. The setting sun lit the western windows, turned them gold, but the others, those not boarded over, were dark, dusty panes, and the barns beyond were already swallowed in shadow.

People back home in Ann Arbor refused to believe there were still folks without electricity in America. When Jill had first come to Ernie's a year and a half ago as a post-graduate student working with experimental bean crops, Ernie had only the diesel generator in the barn for the milking machines and fans. Last winter she had persuaded him to get the electricity connected to the house and barn, although they hadn't yet found the time or money to install outlets or rig up fixtures. Now there were table lamps plugged into extension cords in most of the rooms of the farmhouse, but Ernie, if left to his own devices in the evenings, still sat at the kitchen table with the oil lamp or the Coleman lantern. Jill was always meaning to convince him to play cards with her or mend household appliances and furniture, but he preferred to rest and talk and drink bottles of cheap beer from the grocery. And in the end, she was happy just to read and have the man touch her with those strong hands of his, calloused and infused with wild energy he picked up from fixing tractors and mending fences and birthing calves. She became weak to the point of stupidity under the influence of those hands. Despite their exhaustion, she and Ernie had made love nearly every night through the winter, spring, and summer. Jill did not want to get pregnant—maybe not ever—but she was beginning to fear her birth control pills might not hold up to the frequency and ferocity of their embraces. Ernie already had two kids from his previous marriage, both of whom hated farming.

Jill parked the truck and retied the red handkerchief around her hair, which had gone frizzy from the humidity. A big clapboard house like this Jentzen place could have been a showpiece in the historic district in Ann Arbor, with the siding, trim, and glass all repaired, but out here, rising up from the dark weeds, this turn-of-the-last-century house seemed doomed to collapse. She ascended the steps to the front door and knocked, but the wood was so soft and wet her knuckles made little sound. She might have pushed the door open a few inches and yelled inside, as folks did at her and Ernie's place, but there was no door handle, and the door was shut tight. After a short wait, she ventured around the back and walked up the wooden stairs. The bottom step was rotting through in the middle.

She peered through the screen door and knocked. She studied the lines of the room until she began to make out the silhouette of a shriveled old man in a thin undershirt, sitting motionless at a table. His sunken chest made her want to turn around and walk down the stairs and get into her truck and drive away, but she'd come all the way out here, and she would damn well get that hog, sick or mean as it might be. She made herself knock again. Anyway, it was stupid to think a dead man would be sitting at a table—surely, he was just a skinny old guy with bad hearing. After what seemed like a long time, a woman's voice said, "Come in."

Jill stepped inside the hot, dark kitchen, felt her work boots press grit into the plank floor, yanked her arm back just before it brushed against a big wood-burning cook stove, on top of which a three-gallon pot of water steamed. Although a fire burned in the stove, not even a candle was lit to defend against the oncoming darkness. A woman was standing at a big double sink, facing a boarded-up window with her back to Jill, washing dishes in slow motion. Jill approached her, also in slow motion—the woman had told Jill to come in, hadn't she? Jill allowed her eyes to trace the skirt of the woman's sagging housedress, down to the backs of her thin calves, one of which was marked with a dark, vertical gash. Her canvas shoes had no laces and stretched to accommodate her swollen ankles. Jill felt an urge to tighten up her own bootlace, although it would've hurt.

As her eyes adjusted to the dim light, three more silent men materialized at the table, and a boy. The thick bodies, the big table, the chairs that didn't fit under the table, the stove jutting out—it all made the room feel crowded, as though it would be difficult for her to turn and run if she needed to. Two of the men wore uniform shirts over their gray undershirts, and it was probably the dark that made all their bearded faces seem uniformly grimy. The boy was thin and shirtless in his overalls, maybe thirteen, with dark blond hair stringy from sweat. His mouth hung open, and his panting made Jill think of the way her chickens sweated through their open mouths on the hottest days.

The men all had a forward curve to their shoulders, with their forearms resting on the table as though they were defending bowls of food, only there were no bowls. The man across the table glanced up at her, and Jill raised her arm to wave, but when his eyes settled on her breasts, she changed her mind and crossed her arms instead. Could this guy with the huge fists and slick rubbery forehead be Ernie's old classmate, the kid without a sandwich? The old man with the sunken chest stared into the center of the table, at the empty cutting board and the plaid box of store-brand salt, and Jill wondered if these men were prepared to sit in silence all night until the sun came up. Sometimes Ernie fell asleep sitting in his kitchen chair, his arms folded on the table.

"I'm here about the boar hog. For twenty-five dollars," Jill said. "If you still have it." When she got no immediate response, she began to wonder if she were in the right place. Maybe there were run-down farms like this at the end of every dirt road in the county. "There was a card up at the grocery," Jill said, trying to stay calm.

"Russell, go get the hog for this lady," the woman said without turning. Her voice was slow, rusty, as though speaking were painful.

The boy rose, walked around Jill, and went out the screen door, and its springing shut made almost no noise against the damp doorframe. It had rained practically every day this August, an absurd amount of rain, overflowing ditches, causing Ernie's field pond to swell onto manured land. (Strange to think it was her pond, too, her manured land.) As a result, the pond water was now polluted, and they had to water the cows in the barn, which made for extra work.

"Give me the money," the woman said. She wiped her hands on her housedress and limped over to Jill.

Despite the swollen ankles and two missing teeth, the woman appeared not much older than Jill, maybe thirty-five at the most. Her hair was still a rich brown, but her face was rough, as though sunburned season after season. Jill always tried to remember to put on sunscreen, but rarely reapplied it after sweating it off. The woman held out her raw hand, and as Jill gave her the five and the twenty, she noted her own hand was torn up from scrubbing the cow barn's concrete floors and walls to prepare for this morning's inspection. Jill's gloves had shredded against the concrete, and it would take weeks of medicated lotion before the skin healed. Without ever meeting Jill's gaze, the woman limped back to the sink and resumed her slow-motion dishwashing.

The woman spoke toward her dishes: "You'd better follow Russell out to the pen."

"Thank you, ma'am." Jill backed toward the door, imagining that one of the men might suddenly come to life, awaken from his stupor to reach out and clasp a hand around her leg or arm in a grip strong enough to keep her there. Maybe the woman doing dishes was their prisoner, forced to clean house and to have the men's children—except that she seemed to be in charge. In any case, why weren't there any other women here? Jill pushed on the screen door, noticed at eye level a tear in the screen that had been repaired with black thread in a zigzag pattern. She and Ernie had repaired their screen with duct tape last week, and she had felt bad, thinking about how her father used to replace a porch screen when it had the tiniest hole. Her father couldn't understand how Jill could choose a life where there was no time to relax and do things right. She had failed to convince him that the relaxing and the joy were in the hard work—something she believed most days.

She descended the stairs, sinking into that broken step, but not quite snapping the wood. The air outside should have felt free and clean, but the mood of that kitchen followed her out into the humid evening.

"Russell?" she shouted tentatively and then heard a clatter and a squeal from the direction of the barns. She whispered, "Where the hell are you?"

She followed the trail, cut through burdock, ragweed, and pokeweed, felt the poisonous poke berries smash against her arms and face, to arrive at a pigpen built of old iron-and-wood cement forms wired together. As the pig-shit smell hit her, she saw the dim outline of a skinny, dark hog, up to its belly in mud. She switched on her flashlight and found the batteries were dead. The swampy twelve-by-twelve-foot pen didn't appear to have a weed or a scrap of food in it, and there were no feed or water troughs visible above the soupy muck. By leaning over the west side of the pen, Russell had somehow dragged the pig against the side, gotten a rope around its torso, behind its front legs. The hog had its nose sunk in the mud, and in the dark, its visible eye looked as dull as the eyes of those men in the kitchen, whose presence she still felt like breath on her neck.

She moved around to the back of the hog and saw that one testicle looked swollen. She absentmindedly aimed the dead flashlight and clicked the useless switch. Then she leaned in close to study the hind end of the hog as best she could in shadow. There appeared to be a dark gash on the swollen side of the scrotum. The pig's front legs buckled, and he went to his knees. Mud splattered Jill's chin and lips.

"What happened to his goddamned balls?" Jill took off her handkerchief and wiped her mouth.

"Uncle Roy tried to cut him." The boy spoke in a nasal tone.

"Your uncle tried to castrate a full-grown hog?" Jill should have waited to pay until she'd seen what she was buying, confirmed that this creature was going to do the job she needed done. If her whole pig-roast operation were going to depend on this dull-looking animal, maybe she should say screw it now before wasting any more energy. All along, she and the neighbor had assumed they'd be able to borrow somebody's boar hog for breeding, until they discovered that everybody local was out of the pig business and that they would have to artificially inseminate at thirty bucks a pop. She had been a fool to think the solution would be as cheap and simple as buying this hog. She could still drive away, she thought, forget that twenty-five dollars and let these people and their pig and their house continue to collapse. She could still pour all her energy into corn and soybeans.

"Ma says you can't eat boar meat," the boy said. "It'll poison you."

"He seems awful weak," Jill said.

"We starved him, to make him weak for Uncle Roy to cut him. But he broke his rope, and Uncle Roy got bit, and he told ma he won't try again."

"You're sure he didn't take off his testicles? Because I need him for breeding."

"Ma says if he was castrated we could fatten him and eat him. They're fighting about it all week."

The pig needed only one good testicle to do the job, and Jill knew she was taking the damned pig no matter what the kid said. She supposed they didn't use a veterinarian or anesthesia on the poor fellow. Worst-case scenario, the infection would resist treatment, and she would shoot him and bury the carcass. This is part of what Ernie feared, no doubt, her wasting her money, *their* money. She tried not to resent the way even small amounts of money had to be such a big deal for them.

Early this year, Jill had sunk most of her grandmother's inheritance into expanding and updating the small milking operation, and the rest of it into some experimental oil beans that were going to pay off big, and now she no longer had enough money to buy anything more than a candy bar on impulse. Ernie had only reluctantly gone along with displacing a hundred acres of soy with Jill's experimental beans, which in the end had never sprouted because of a June freeze. When her parents sent her fifty bucks last week, she'd thought she'd use it to replace one of the milk-stall stanchions that was rusting through, but then the rumor started around that the dairy was going to stop buying milk from small producers in the coming year. When she'd proposed expanding the milk barn and herd this past spring, Ernie had initially resisted. When their neighbor reported the rumor, six months later, that they would soon be out of the dairy business, Ernie nodded and kept nodding. When Jill finally looked him in the eye, she saw he felt sorry for her. She looked away from him, went into the kitchen and ate the entire quart of blackcap raspberries she was planning to use for making jam. Later that day, her hands and mouth still purple, she decided they should be in the pig-roasting business.

Jill had no intention of eating this particular hog at this time, but she had been doing a lot of reading on the subject of pork, and she thought this kid's ma and a lot of people might be wrong about boar meat. Boar meat was usually fine—although the flavor might be slightly tainted in older boars, especially those with unhealthy diets—and some new-age farmers said the whole notion of boar taint was an old wives' tale. On the other hand, some who had experienced the tainted flavor said it made them swear off pork forever.

"Can you help me get him in the trailer?" Jill asked. She held out a five-dollar bill.

The boy made an awful sound to clear his throat. She thought he was going to spit, but he swallowed and stared dully at the money. Jill wondered if she ought to check with the authorities, make sure the kid was going to school, as her sister the social worker would have. Reporting folks to the authorities was frowned upon in these parts, however, by Ernie as much as anybody. "It's awful easy to make trouble for people," Ernie had said on more than one occasion. Jill wondered how long people could survive being this poor, how many generations.

She leaned close to the boy, pushed the five-dollar bill into his front overall pocket, saw how his tanned skin was streaked with dirt and sweat. He stared at her, open mouthed, as if waiting for directions.

"Go on, get him out," she said finally. "I'll get the trailer up here."

The boy untwisted some wire and wiggled loose one of the heavy iron forms, showing he was stronger than he looked. Jill returned to her truck and backed the trailer in, relying on the taillights to get as close as she dared without taking a chance on running over something that would flatten her tires.

It took them a while to maneuver the slow, muddy hog down the path and into the trailer in the dark, mostly pushing from behind, picking him up when he fell, feeling hip bones and ribs through rough skin, avoiding the swollen testicle. Both the boy and the hog stepped on Jill's bruised foot, and when they got the hog up the ramp in the dark, he fell over onto his side. The two had to use all their strength to push him in the last few inches to close up the gate.

"Don't you have any brothers or sisters?" Jill asked, wiping her hands on her jeans. The boy shrugged, or maybe he didn't respond at all. He was already walking away toward the house, disappearing into the tall weeds.

Once she got her wheels back in the two-track ruts, she was on automatic pilot. Neither speeding up nor slowing down diminished the violent bouncing of the stock trailer, and Jill supposed it didn't matter if her eyes blurred. Although her mud-crusted hands smelled of pig shit, she picked up the chocolate bar from the seat beside her. She had meant to open it when she was clean and fed; she had meant to unfold the wrapper and foil carefully, to break off one piece each night. Then she would carefully refold the glossy paper and gold foil to retain the original shape and tuck the bar away in her dresser drawer, repeating the ritual until it was gone. Instead she tore away the wrapper with her fingers and teeth, undressed the top of the chocolate bar, spit out bits of foil. She bit into the heat-softened chocolate and chewed and swallowed wildly. The luxury of it made her feel drunk. She tore away the rest of the wrapper and devoured the whole damned thing. Despite the pig stink, it tasted better than anything she'd eaten lately, and it was gone way too soon. The memory of that taste then became an ache in her chest.

When it began to rain, as it was apparently going to do every day for the rest of her life, Jill rolled up her window, trapped herself inside the cab with mosquitoes that buzzed around her face and ears. The hog still lay flat on its side in the trailer, its head and limbs bouncing like meat—it hadn't moved since its collapse. Her family was right: just because she'd studied agriculture for six years didn't mean she knew a damned thing about farming. All she'd ever wanted, from the time she was a kid, was to work with land and animals, to work beside a good man, but there was so much more to it. Her father had said that her marrying Ernie was proof positive she didn't know a damned thing about real life. Her father couldn't understand how Ernie's calmness might be the antidote to everything uneasy about her; he didn't see how the contours of the farm interlocked precisely with the contours of her mind.

Her father might enjoy leaning back in his office chair about now and telling her she'd wasted twenty-five—no, thirty—dollars and a quarter-tank of gas. Until Jill had seen the Jentzen woman, she hadn't understood what her family feared for her. She'd known that, like all the farmers in this downward spiral, she and Ernie could lose everything, but she'd hoped her ideas for extra income could postpone the end indefinitely. Maybe she was, instead, hurrying the end along.

As she pulled into Ernie's driveway, their driveway, she crumpled the chocolate bar wrapper so it would be unidentifiable as something fancy, except that no matter how small she crushed it, the foil glistened in the moonlight coming through the windshield. She finally shoved it into her pants pocket, although the effort caused her to swerve. When she turned off the engine, the boar was silent and still as a pork roast, beaten by the trailer's bouncing and by the hard rain, which had started and stopped twice. At least the corpse would be clean, she told herself.

Ernie was sitting at the porch picnic table with the Coleman lantern, moths fluttering and crashing against the glass. He and the neighbor were sorting through a box of old leather harness parts she'd dragged down the stairs yesterday. Atop the table sat the neighbor's acne-studded son. All three kept looking at her and the trailer. The boy, sixteen this summer, was dressed in jeans and a rock-and-roll T-shirt. He was a helpful kid, although when Ernie wasn't there he sometimes sighed at her and stood too close. Between taking sips of beer from the bottle in his left hand, the boy was swatting mosquitoes with his right. Ernie looked at her expectantly, but she didn't want to get out of the truck. There was no point in getting out and showing Ernie the pig—he knew, had known all along, what folly this was.

"So how's your hog?" Ernie said. She was surprised she heard his voice from the porch so clearly, as though he were sitting in the truck beside her. He sounded almost enthusiastic.

"Them Jentzens still living on woodchuck meat and dandy-lion greens?" the neighbor shouted good-humoredly. The neighbor had lost about everything except his house and garage in the last few years. His farm, once bigger than Ernie's (although not as beautiful, with fewer stands of trees and no watering pond with turtles, no stream to rinse your face in, and too few blackcap raspberries), had been sold by the bank to a larger corporate farm. He now drove forty minutes each way to work at the new Tractor Supply store off the highway. But he had gotten the runt gilts as piglets for free somewhere, and he could butcher a pig like nobody's business, she knew, and he still had a stainless steel pig smoker, presentable enough for any sort of graduation or anniversary party.

"The hog's dead," Jill said, more harshly than she'd intended. Ernie nodded. The neighbor nodded, took a drink of beer. The son glanced at his father, took a drink of his own beer. Jill was grateful her sister the social worker wasn't there to see it.

Ernie approached, carrying the Coleman lantern, squatted down, and took a close look at the inert hog. After a minute or so, he came up and stood beside the driver's door.

"Looks like he's been shot," Ernie said. "But he isn't dead."

"Shot?" Jill said. "He was starved and got an infection. I was too late—" She had almost added, *to save him.*

"An old bullet wound in his chest, almost healed over. Do you suppose that's how the Jentzens caught him?"

Jill shrugged.

Ernie didn't swat at the mosquitoes, but let them draw out what blood they would from his exposed face and neck and arms. He lifted Jill's hand off the edge of the window to hold it, and that sent energy through her arm, down into her belly and her legs— only she didn't want to desire him now. She wanted to unhook the trailer, pull out of this driveway, and head south until she was far enough away that she could look back and see it all in miniature, see all her farm schemes as comic failures. Once she was far away, she would take a deep breath and ask herself if she belonged here at all—maybe her whole time with Ernie was nothing more than a crazy adventure.

"Jentzens got a good crop of pokeweed this year?" Ernie asked and jiggled her hand. Jill glanced in the sideview mirror to see her face was smeared with purple. She felt him staring at her with the same fierce admiration he showed when she lifted the other end of something heavy or dressed a wound on a heifer or produced some compelling information about soy yields. But did he see her as a farmer? she wondered. What would her father say if he were here? Would he make clever remarks about failing farms and inbred families at the ends of dirt roads where everybody had six fingers on each hand? She pulled her hand out of Ernie's to swipe at a mosquito on her forearm and smeared the blood across her skin. She wiped her forehead and cheeks to get rid of any mosquitoes she might not be feeling, and she smelled the pig shit on her hands.

Ernie moved back to the trailer and squatted down to study the pig. He held his lantern near the animal's face and spoke, or at least his mouth was moving, as he reached through the slats and felt the pig's neck and chest.

Jill couldn't be sure from his reflection in the sideview mirror, but he seemed to be talking to the hog. She couldn't bring herself to turn around and face him, but sat listening, resenting the scuffing and murmuring of the neighbor and his son. She adjusted the mirror for a better view. Ernie had a way of doing things; he made hooking up a cow to a milking machine or rebuilding a tractor carburetor seem as natural as letting water flow down a hill.

From the trailer, there was a snort and a scraping sound. In the mirror, she saw the dark hog thrusting up its shoulders and dragging itself onto its knees, back legs, and finally its quivering front legs.

"Holy motherfucker," Jill shouted and stretched halfway out the truck window to see. Ernie laughed. For some reason he found it hilarious whenever Jill swore, as she sometimes did in bed. Once upright, the pig snorked a complaint, supported itself by leaning against the side of the trailer, and jammed its fist-sized snout between two boards.

The neighbor raised his beer bottle, shouted, "Lazarus arises!" and stepped off the porch. The son raised his beer alongside. Jill slid out of the truck, left the door hanging open, but at her approach, her husband stood and stopped what he'd been doing.

"Were you saying something to him?" Jill asked.

"Nothing much." Ernie shrugged.

"He's one ugly son of a bitch," the neighbor said, sidling up to Jill. The son approached and stood right behind her. She felt him looming—how tall was that kid going to get?

She had assumed the hog was black, but the rain had rinsed away the mud. In the lantern light he looked the color of dried blood, deeper toned than her Duroc gilts. His shoulders and head were bristled like a wild hog, and pointed tusks stuck out from his lower jaw. How could she not have noticed those tusks back at the Jentzen farm?

The neighbor laughed and said, "He's smelling those gilts now—that's what's got Lazarus arising. You'd better tell our sweet girl piggies to hold onto their piggy panties."

The men and the boy couldn't stop staring at the hog, and the four male bodies boxed Jill in, put her a little closer to all of them than she wanted to be. Her foot was throbbing now.

The pig had been dull at that farm, lifeless in that trailer. Was the smell of those gilts in the barn so strong as to drag him back from the dead?

"Maybe this is something that got mixed up with one of those wild hogs they got down south in the state," Ernie said. "Or maybe he got loose from the state fair—they got those big show pigs."

Jill didn't know how the pig could have looked so much less formidable back in its mud pen. She'd had her hands all over this pig, pushing it into the trailer, and it had seemed smaller.

"No telling how the Jentzens ended up with this thing," the neighbor said. "Probably they just caught it up and put it in an old pen. Remember, they used to have pigs when we was kids."

"Some kid out shooting squirrels might've taken pot shots at it," Ernie said. "Look at his skin here, feel here, underneath, you can feel a twenty-two bullet. Right there." Ernie lifted the lantern.

"I'll be damned," said the neighbor, feeling the hog's chest. "Is that another one in his leg?"

"Doesn't look like he's been fed in a while, though," Ernie said. "We'd better get some corn in him."

"Hey, one of his nuts is swelled up," the boy said. "That's one dang big nut."

"It's infected," Jill said. The pig was standing still for the men's handling, not biting, not fussing. "We'll get him on antibiotics."

"That's a big old nut, all right," the neighbor said. "Bigger'n a baseball."

"Bigger'n a softball," the boy said.

"Can we cut the tusks off?" Jill asked

"Not sure how you go about cutting tusks off a full grown fellow like him. There'd be a lot of blood." The neighbor was close enough that Jill smelled his beer breath, stronger than the pig scent. She smelled the boy too, his sharp sweat. She reached for her husband's hand, but brushed her knuckles against the hot lantern glass instead and recoiled. She had asked the Jentzen kid about sisters. What about aunts? A grandmother? She should have demanded an answer: Why had there been no other women at that farm? And, more importantly, why had the one woman stayed?

Jill stepped back, away from the men, inhaled the clean, damp air, and released her shoulders. She had built the new hog pen to the neighbor's specifications: posts driven down four feet, woven wire buried underground to prevent digging, sides six feet high, a double thickness of two-by-fours, nailed and then screwed. One corner had a shelter from weather, and another corner had a squeeze pen, where she could trap and medicate animals. She had the medicines and ointments to nurse this weak monster back to strength in time for the gilts to become fertile at about 220 days. With six breeding females, each birthing ten piglets per litter, two litters a year, and with these men to help her, this plan was once again looking very promising. This boar had turned out to be exactly what she needed, a creature even bullets could not stop.

Acknowledgments

Heidi Bell, Carla Vissers, Andy Mozina, and Lisa Lenzo are the best friends a writer could have, and these stories sing their praises. Christopher Magson's good humor and good husbandry have made the book possible, and Jaimy Gordon has wised it up. Thank you, Melissa Fraterrigo, Rachael Perry, and Donna Sparkman for going carefully through the collection. Various stories (and my writing life) are better because of Susan Ramsey, Jamie Blake, Gina Betcher, Glenn Deutsch, Shawn Wagner, Elizabeth Kerlikowske, David Dodd Lee, Tom Campbell, George Campbell, Loring Janes, Jaci Dillon, John Weaver, and Don York, and of course Susanna. The events and characters depicted in these pages are fictional, but my hometown of Comstock, Michigan, where many of these stories could have taken place, is very real.

Gratefully acknowledged are the magazines in which these stories originally appeared: "The Trespasser" appeared in *Witness;* "The Yard Man," "The Inventor, 1972," and "Fuel for the Millennium" appeared in *The Southern Review,* and "The Inventor, 1972" won the 2009 Eudora Welty Prize for Fiction; "World of Gas" appeared in *The Heartlands Today;* "The Solutions to Brian's Problem" appeared in *Diagram;* "Family Reunion" appeared in *Mid-American Review* and was originally read aloud and broadcast on a WBEZ Program, *Stories on Stage;* "Winter Life" and "Falling" appeared in *Alaska Quarterly Review;* "Bringing Belle Home" appeared in *ACM;* "King Cole's American Salvage" appeared in *Plaiedes;* "The

Burn" appeared in *Controlled Burn;* "Storm Warning" appeared in *Orchid: A Literary Review;* "Boar Taint" appeared in *The Kenyon Review.*